HIDDEN AGENDA

A SAM PRICHARD MYSTERY

HIDDEN AGENDA

DAVID ARCHER

USA TODAY BESTSELLING AUTHOR

Hidden Agenda

Copyright © 2017 by David Archer.

All right reserved.

Published by: David Archer

1

There's something to be said for sleeping in, and Sam Prichard was the kind of guy who would take advantage of every opportunity to do so. Since school had just let out for the summer and nobody had to be anywhere early in the morning, Sam hadn't even bothered to set an alarm.

Of course, the best-laid plans of mice and men, as they say...

Sam was awakened by the sound of his phone ringing and threw out a hand to find the blasted thing on his nightstand. "Hello," he mumbled into the phone.

"Sam, before you say anything, I want you to know this isn't my fault," he heard his mother say. "I'm just the messenger, remember that, okay?"

Sam groaned. "Just spit it out, Mom," he said. He held the phone out and let one eye focus on the time. It was just after seven. He held the phone back to his ear.

"Okay," Grace said with a sigh. "It's Beauregard. Kim came out of her room this morning for breakfast and said Beauregard wanted me to call you. I'm supposed to tell you to take the case."

Beauregard was, according to Indie's mother Kim, the ghost of a confederate soldier who acted as her "spirit guide," giving her advice, which she sometimes needed to pass on to others. Sam thought he was an alter ego Kim had created to mask her own ability to see bits and pieces of the future, but he never said that to her face; Indie had warned him that it could be too hard for her mom to accept, so he pretended to believe in the old ghost at least part of the time.

Sam blinked, trying to wake up enough to understand what was going on. "Take what case?" he asked. "I haven't had any new calls."

"All I know is that she insists that *he* says you have to take the case. You know how Beauregard is, he doesn't give you any details. Just these vague hints, and I don't know what they mean."

Indie rolled over and leaned up on an elbow to look at his face. "Beauregard?" she whispered.

Sam nodded. "Okay, I guess," he said into the phone. "Personally I think Beauregard is a load of hogwash, but I have to admit he's saved my life a time or two. The next case that comes my way, I'll take it no matter how silly it sounds. Good enough?"

He could hear Grace speaking to Kim, who rented a

room from her. A moment later she came back on the line. "I guess Beauregard says that's okay. Did I wake you guys up?"

"Yeah, we were kind of sleeping," Sam said. "Don't worry about it, though, we'll be okay. What are you up to today?"

"Well, I've got to go and write a couple of new listings today, but I think Kim was planning on coming over to your place. That's why she wanted me to call you this morning, so she wouldn't have to be the one to tell you about that crazy old soldier of hers."

"She's getting smarter, then," Sam said, and Indie poked him in the ribs. "Oof!"

"Well, I won't keep bending your ear. Tell Indie and Kenzie I said hi, and I'll see them this afternoon."

"I will." Sam ended the call and set the phone back on the nightstand. "Beauregard says I have to take the case," he said to Indie. "It'd be nice if I knew what case he meant."

"Maybe he does mean the next one. Let's wait and see if it's one you'd normally turn down." She tossed off the covers and rolled to her feet, shaking her nightgown to make it fall modestly around her. "Get your lazy butt up and I'll make you bacon and eggs," she said playfully.

"With coffee?" Sam asked, but she was already walking out of the bedroom. He groaned again and got up, sliding into a pair of jeans and then pulling a t-shirt over his head before following her to the kitchen.

Kenzie, their not-quite-six-year-old daughter, came running down the stairs. "Is it time to get up yet?" she asked, and Sam scooped her up with one arm to carry her the rest of the way. They had told her not to get out of bed until they were up, and she had been lying up there listening for any sounds for more than an hour.

"Yep," he told her. "And Mommy's making us bacon and eggs!"

Kenzie's face lit up. "I like bacon," she said, and her cat, whose name was Samson, chose that moment to come tumbling down the stairs. Samson had suffered from distemper as a kitten, and while he had been lucky enough to survive, his coordination hadn't. His back end had a tendency to pass his front end, but even the regular rolls down the stairs didn't seem to hurt him any.

"I think Samson likes it, too," Sam laughed, as the cat followed its own tail into the kitchen ahead of them. He plopped Kenzie into a chair and got her a glass of orange juice, then poured some for himself and Indie.

"Hey," he said as he sat down across from her, "Grandma Kim is coming over later, and Grandma Grace will be here sometime after that. They want to come see you."

The little girl nodded. "Yeah, we're gonna play games and stuff."

"Ooh," Indie said, "that sounds like fun. Maybe I

can—"

She was cut off by the ringing of the office phone, an extension of which was in the dining room. She hurried over to answer it. "Sam Prichard, Private Investigator," she said.

Indie listened for a moment, and then turned to look at Sam with eyebrows that were threatening to climb over her forehead. "Um, yes," she said. "We'll expect you at ten."

She hung up the phone a moment later and walked back into the kitchen, where the bacon in the skillet was just beginning to sizzle. "That was a girl named Heather Biggs," she said. "She wants to talk to you about finding her mother, who she says has been abducted."

Sam's eyebrows were climbing a bit as well. "Abducted? That sounds like a matter for the police, not a private eye."

"She says the police don't believe her," Indie said, "and neither does her father or her stepdad or anyone else, but she's certain she's right and needs help. And there's one other thing, Sam—she's only fourteen years old."

"Fourteen?" Sam echoed, aghast. "I can't..."

"Sam," Indie said. "Remember Beauregard? You said you'd take the next case, no matter what, right? And this is definitely one you'd normally turn down, isn't it?"

"Well, yes, but..." His eyes stared into those of his

wife. "Oh, you've gotta be kidding. This can't be what Kim meant, can it?"

Indie shrugged her shoulders as she flipped the bacon. "It fits," she said. "I think you better at least hear the girl out and agree to look into it, don't you?"

Sam scowled. "I guess so," he said. "What did you say her name was, Biggs?"

"Yeah."

Sam got up and went back to the bedroom to get his cell phone, dialing it as he came back into the kitchen. It was answered as he took his chair again.

"Denver Police, this is Sergeant Ragsdale, how can I help you?"

"Sergeant, this is Sam Prichard. Have you got a missing persons case on a woman named Biggs?"

The desk sergeant sighed. "It's actually Jensen, but I know who you mean. Her daughter's name is Biggs, and she's been calling every hour for the past day and a half, even at night. That case is with Detective Lemmons, let me transfer you."

Sam heard the hold music come on, but it lasted only a few seconds. "Detective Lemmons."

"Jerry? Sam Prichard. You've got the missing persons on Jensen?"

"Yep," Jerry Lemmons said. He and Sam had once worked together in the Vice Division, and knew each other fairly well. "Don't tell me you're being dragged into this, too."

"Actually, I got a call from a potential client who says the woman was abducted, but that you don't think so. Any truth to that?"

Jerry laughed. "Let me guess, the daughter called you? Listen, Sam, this is a simple case of a momma who didn't want to be a momma anymore. I've got cell phone records, credit card records and a ton more info that says she's been having an affair for the past couple months, and now she and Romeo have run off together. The kid doesn't want to believe that of course, but it's pretty clear."

"Do you know who Romeo is?" Sam asked. "Any trace of him?"

"Yeah, he's Martin Fletcher. Won't be the first time he's seduced a married woman and got her to run off, but they always come back after a few weeks. Soon as her money runs out, he'll dump her in Boise or somewhere. She'll call home and beg for help and forgiveness, they always do."

Sam closed his eyes and thought for a second. "Jerry, are you sure about this? Is there any chance there really could be something nefarious about this one?"

"You want to see the motel security video of the two of them going into the room together? I'm sure, Sam, it's a runaway mother situation. Nothing more than that."

Sam sighed into the phone. "Okay. I'll talk to you later."

He ended the call and tossed the phone onto the table beside his plate. "That was Jerry Lemmons, guy I knew back in Vice. He's got the case and says it's just a matter of a mother who's run off with a boyfriend. According to him, everything from her cell phone records to motel security videos backs that up." Indie just looked at him without saying anything. "Okay, I know what I said. I'm not gonna blow the girl off, don't worry. I just don't know what to do with a case that isn't really what she thinks it is."

Indie smiled at him. "Maybe the idea is to help her come to grips with reality," she said. "Sometimes kids have a hard time with that."

"Yeah, I know," Sam said. "We'll just have to wait and see."

They finished breakfast with Kenzie and were just sitting down in the living room with her to watch some TV when Sam's mother dropped Kim off. Sam opened the door for his mother-in-law, and Kenzie ran to give the woman a hug.

"Good," Indie said. "Now that you're here, you can keep Kenzie entertained while Sam and I interview a new client. She should be here in about fifteen minutes, so your timing is perfect."

Kim smiled and nodded. "Yes," she said. "Beauregard says this is the one you've got to take. He says there are three lives to be saved and only Sam can do it."

Sam looked at her intently. "Three lives to save? That's more info than he usually gives. Is there anything else?"

Kim shrugged her shoulders and kept her eyes on her granddaughter. "Only that you'll have a hard time figuring out who to believe. You'll have to trust your own instincts, no matter how crazy you think they are."

Sam stood there in the middle of the room for a long moment, just looking at Kim and imagining the old soldier standing right behind her, then shook his head as the two of them turned to head down the hall to their bedroom. They changed into fresh clothes and then went to the office that was tucked behind his garage.

"Believe it or not," Sam said as Indie took the chair at her desk, "I've suddenly got a feeling this case is for real. Old Beauregard doesn't usually give me any hints, but this one sounds kind of serious."

"Yeah," Indie said. "I got a chill when Mom said he told her you need to save three lives. I wonder whose."

There was a knock on the outer office door, and Indie got up to open it. A young girl who didn't look like she'd even made it to fourteen yet stepped inside.

"Heather?" Indie asked, and the girl nodded.

"Yeah," she said. "I called a little while ago..."

"Yes, that was me you talked to. This is my

husband, Sam. Why don't you sit down there in the chair and tell us what this is all about?"

Heather ducked her head shyly and took the chair Indie had offered. Indie sat down in the one beside her.

"I know you're gonna think I'm crazy," Heather said after a moment, "but I'm not. I know my mom, and she wouldn't run out on me the way they say she did. The only way she'd disappear is if she got kidnapped."

"Okay," Sam said. "First, why don't you tell me what's happened, and then tell me why you think the police are wrong."

Heather had kept her eyes down on the floor before, but now she raised them up to look into Sam's own. "Mom didn't come home from work three days ago," she said. "The cops told my stepdad she was having an affair and ran off with her boyfriend, but that isn't true. Mom told me about Marty, and she wasn't his girlfriend. He worked with her at the auto parts store, but he got himself in some kind of trouble and she was trying to help him get it all straightened out. It was something about something he knew that other people didn't want him to know, and he was scared somebody was gonna kill him, so she was helping him hide 'til they could figure out what to do."

Sam's eyes were wide, and he noticed Indie's looked about the same. "Heather, did you tell the police about this?"

She nodded her head. "Yeah, but they say Marty

even gonna get married, once."

Indie looked at Sam curiously, but didn't say a word. Sam looked confused for a moment, and then his eyes narrowed. "Heather," he said slowly, "what is your mother's name?"

"It's Tracy," the girl answered. "Tracy Jensen, now, but it used to be Tracy—"

"Prentiss," Sam said. "Tracy Prentiss." He looked over at Indie and smiled halfheartedly. "She was my closest friend all the way through school, and we got engaged just before she went off to New York for college, but then—well, things just changed, and we ended up calling it off. I haven't really even spoken to her since then, I don't think."

"What happened was that she got pregnant with me," Heather said, glancing at Indie. "Mom said it was an accident at a party, but she ended up marrying my dad. They got a divorce three years ago, and Mom married my stepdad last year." She turned back to Sam. "Gary's okay, my stepdad, but he's always afraid Mom is gonna get tired of him, cause he's a lot older than she is."

Sam nodded slowly. "And she told you to come to me if she disappeared?"

Nodding again, Heather said, "Yeah. She said she read about you being a private detective, now, and that if anything happened to her, you were the only person who might be willing to help." The girl looked down at the small purse she was carrying and opened it, taking out an envelope that she held out toward Sam. "I don't have a lot of money, but I've got these. They were from my grandpa's baseball card collection. I know they're worth something, and I'll give 'em to you if you'll try to find her for me."

Sam glanced at the envelope but didn't reach for it. "Heather, we're not going to worry about money right now," he said, and Indie chimed in with, "Of course we're not. Sam will find her, you just count on it!"

Sam cleared his throat. "Actually, I was going to say that I'll do my best to find her," he said, "but I can't guarantee anything. If the police are right, then she'll probably call home sometime soon in any case, but the fact that she told you to come to me makes me think she might have gotten into something worse than that, so I'll see what I can find out."

"I told you," Heather said, "you can't trust the cops. Some of them are in on whatever it is she was worried about. She told me if I came to you, to make sure I told you not to trust the cops."

Sam looked at Indie for a moment, then back to Heather. "Okay, I won't," he said. "You said your mom worked at a parts store?"

"Yeah, Rocky Mountain Auto Parts. She's the assistant manager there. She used to be a nurse, but this pays better, she says. She's been there for a little over three years, now."

"Okay," Sam said, making notes. "What about her friends? Who might know something about what she's doing?"

Heather shrugged. "She doesn't really have many friends. She mostly just hangs out at home or at church when she isn't working. I think her best friend is probably Mrs. Raymond, the lady who lives next door to us, but they just sit around and talk sometimes is all. They don't go out and do anything, and I don't think Mom would ever tell her anything important. Mrs. Raymond is a big gossip, Mom says."

"What's your address, Heather?" The girl gave it to him, and he got the address for Mrs. Raymond as well, then added Heather's cell number to his notes. "Okay, let me see what I can find out, and I'll try to let you know something pretty soon. I can't promise anything, but I'll do my best to get to the bottom of this, all right?"

The girl smiled for the first time. "Mom said you would," she said. "She said if nobody else would help me, you would." She suddenly bounced to her feet and ran around Sam's desk to kiss his cheek, then smiled sheepishly at Indie as she hurried out the door. Indie watched as she climbed onto a bicycle and rode away, then looked back at Sam.

"So," she said with a mock scowl on her face. "Your ex-fiancé is in trouble, and sends her kid to call you for help?"

Sam rolled his eyes. "Indie, I haven't heard anything from Tracy since the 'Dear John' letter that told me she was breaking up with me to marry the guy who knocked her up. She sent back my ring and that was it. I think the only time I even saw her since then was back when my ex dragged me to a rummage sale one Saturday, and she was there buying old dishes. She looked up at me, we said hi, and then she paid for her stuff and left."

"I'm not jealous, Sam," Indie said, letting a smile spread. "I'm just thinking how odd it is that Beauregard says you have to take the very next case, and it turns out to be your ex-girlfriend's teenage daughter who comes to the office." She leaned forward and put her elbows on his desk. "So, what do you really think about this one?"

"The thing that troubles me is that Tracy must have honestly thought she could be in danger. That's the only reason I can think of to tell Heather to come to me if anything happened to her. That doesn't sound to me like she was in some kind of romantic entanglement, does it to you?"

Indie shook her head. "No," she said. "It sounds like someone who tried to help a friend and got into something over her head. You know what worries me?"

"What?"

"Beauregard said you have to save three lives. What if it's Tracy, Marty and Heather's lives we're talking

15

about? That kid is scared, Sam, scared for her mom, but I think she's a bit scared of what's gonna happen when you start asking questions, too."

Sam sighed. "Well, I can start with Tracy's co-workers," he said. "She and Martin both worked there, so it's possible one of them might have some idea of what was going on. I'll head out there in a minute, and you might start digging into anything you can find on Martin Fletcher. There's bound to be something in the PD files on him."

Indie nodded. "I'll put Herman to work on it now," she said. Herman was a computer program she had written that could hack into most computer systems and databases, searching out information according to rules she entered into it. Before meeting Sam, Indie had been a rising star in the world of hackers, and she now used her talents to help him solve the incredibly difficult cases that seemed to always come his way. "With any luck, I can find his bank, phone and social media accounts, and those might give me some kind of clue about what kind of trouble he might have fallen into."

Sam grinned at her. "Have I mentioned today that I love you?" he asked.

"Not nearly enough."

2

Sam left the house a few minutes later, climbed into his Corvette and drove out to East Colfax Avenue, where Rocky Mountain Auto Parts was located. Sam had once been a regular customer of the store, back when he was working steadily on restoring the 'Vette, but that had been before Tracy would have worked there. The store specialized in performance and custom parts.

He parked in front of the building and got out of the car, his bad hip making him wince as he walked up to the door. A customer coming out held it open for him, and Sam offered his thanks as he stepped inside. A young man behind the counter looked up and smiled.

"Welcome to Rocky Mountain," he said. "I'm Clayton, how can I help you today?"

Sam produced his ID and flashed it. "Sam Prichard," he said. "I'm a private investigator. I was hoping you might be able to tell me something about Tracy Jensen's disappearance."

Clayton's smile got even wider. "Mr. Prichard," he said, "it's an honor to meet you. I follow you on Twitter, man, you're the best private eye since Mickey Spillane!" He extended a hand, and Sam shook it with a smile.

"Well, thanks," he said. "Twitter? That must be something my wife does, I'm not all that into computers."

"Well, she does it great! I love reading about your cases and how you solve them. That last one, with the Army dog who helped you catch the killer? That was awesome!"

Sam grinned, but made a mental note to speak to Indie about Twitter. "Thanks, I appreciate it. As I was saying, though, I'm looking into Ms. Jensen's disappearance, and I was wondering if you can tell me anything that might help."

Clayton toned down his smile a bit and leaned across the counter conspiratorially. "Way I got it, her and Marty Fletcher ran off together," he said softly. "They were always huddling back in the racks, whispering to each other. I think they were having a fling, know what I mean?"

Sam nodded. "Yeah, that's what the police think, too," he said, "but I'm not so sure. Seems Marty may have gotten himself into some kind of trouble, and

Tracy was trying to help him get out of it. Had you heard anything about that?"

Clayton frowned. "I didn't," he said, "but James might have." He leaned back away from Sam and called out. "James? Can you come up here a minute?"

Another man stepped out from between the racks of parts and came toward them. "I'm James, the manager," he said as he got close. "How can I help you, Sir?"

Sam showed his ID again. "Sam Prichard," he said. "I'm looking into Tracy Jensen's disappearance. Wondered if you might have any insight into what may have caused it."

James glanced at Clayton, then motioned for Sam to follow him. "Come on back to my office," he said. "Maybe we'd better talk there."

Sam followed the man through the racks and into a small office that was barely big enough for the desk and two chairs it contained. James took the one behind the desk, and Sam sat in the other. The manager looked at him for a moment, then rose again and shut the door.

"Do you know Marty or Tracy?" he asked.

"I knew Tracy years ago," Sam said without adding anything further. "I've never met Marty Fletcher, but I understand he was in some kind of trouble, and Tracy was trying to help him out of it. Would you know anything about that?"

James seemed to hesitate for a moment, then leaned a bit closer and spoke softly. "Way I got it, Marty was doing one of his YouTube videos, and ended up pissing off some powerful people. He actually claimed he was scared someone was gonna kill him, and I guess Tracy was trying to help him get it all straightened out."

Sam raised an eyebrow. "YouTube videos?"

James scowled. "Yeah, he was always making these videos, where he basically just runs his mouth about something, and I guess people like to hear what he's got to say. Lately, it's been stuff to do with politics a lot, and I told him more than once I better not find him talking up his crap to our customers. He was always going on and on about how the government is corrupt, or how the cops are dirty, that kind of stuff, and I didn't need our store to be associated with it, right? I even told him he couldn't make any more of them in our parking lot."

"He was making videos here?" Sam asked.

James seemed to want to look elsewhere for a moment, but then turned his eyes back to Sam. "He made them in his van," he said. "If you look at a lot of those video rants people do on YouTube, a lot of them are done in cars. I guess it makes 'em seem more real or something, from what Marty said. Anyway, he was making them in our parking lot and I made him stop."

"And you think he got into some kind of trouble? Any idea what kind?"

"Not really," James said. "Way I understood it, he must've said something that made people mad, but I can't really imagine anyone would want to kill him over it, y'know? That sounds like pure paranoia to me."

Sam nodded his understanding. "I can see how it would, yeah. Still, if he made the wrong people angry, I suppose it's possible he could be looking at some kind of dire consequences. Any idea who it might have been?"

James shook his head. "Not a clue," he said. "All I know is he was worried somebody might be after him, and he got Tracy mixed up in it. He disappeared about ten days before she did, but I got the impression she was hiding him out in some motel room and taking food to him after work every day. Then she didn't show up for work day before yesterday, and the cops showed up that afternoon asking about her and Marty. They seem to think the two of 'em were havin' a fling and ran off together, but I can't help wondering if maybe something bad really has happened to the pair of them."

Sam nodded thoughtfully. "If Marty was making political videos and actually aiming them at particular politicians or cops, I can see how he might be worried about repercussions. But afraid of getting killed? Did he have something on someone, something that proved some kind of corruption?"

"Not a clue," James said. "I never paid a lot of attention to his rants, and I didn't let him talk that crap around here at all. Tracy tried to tell me what was going on a few days ago, but to be honest, I didn't want to hear it and I shut her down. It was bad enough trying to deal with our customers who followed him; they were always coming in and asking him about his latest video. I made him tell all of them he wasn't allowed to talk about it here, but I'm sure he did whenever I wasn't around."

"So, he made somebody mad, and then he disappeared," Sam said. "You haven't heard anything from him since then?"

James shook his head. "Not since he just didn't show up for work. That was just about two weeks ago, maybe a little less, and the funny thing was there was a couple of cops here asking about him that morning just when he should have been coming in. He never showed up, though, so they left. All I got after that was Tracy saying he was hiding and wouldn't be back 'til it all got straightened out."

Sam's eyes narrowed, but he simply smiled. "Well, listen," he said. "I really appreciate this. I may need to come back and ask some more questions later, would that be okay?"

"Sure. Anytime."

Sam left the store and got back into his car, pulling his phone from his pocket as he drove out of the parking lot. He dialed Indie's cell number as he drove sedately up the street.

"Hey, Babe," he said when she answered. "Looks like Marty was one of those guys who do videos that go viral, always complaining about the government and such. The way his boss understood it, he got some local politicians or cops mad at him, and even said he was afraid someone was out to kill him. Somehow or other, Tracy was trying to help him get out of whatever mess he was into, and might have been hiding him at a motel."

"Well, that would account for the security video," Indie said. "I let Herman go into the city's database and find everything he could on both Marty and Tracy, so I've got all their cell numbers, credit card numbers and such. Marty's phone went inactive about a week ago, but Tracy was calling him two or three times a day, usually around the same time each day. I took a look at her calls after that, and found another number she was calling around the same times."

"Probably a throwaway phone," Sam said. "She bought him one of those cheap ones and most likely tossed his usual one out on the highway somewhere."

"Yeah, exactly what I figured. Unfortunately, I have no idea who the carrier is—it's one of those that piggybacks on other carriers—so I can't get into any of its records. All I know is that Tracy called it four times the night she disappeared, each call lasting only a few seconds, like she got voicemail. They were also very close together, like only five minutes or so apart. Sort of looks like they might have been frantic calls."

"What about since then? Is Tracy's phone still

active?"

"Doesn't look like it," Indie replied. "It hasn't made any calls since the last of those four calls to the disposable. I tried getting a GPS trace on it, but it's not even showing up anywhere."

"Gotcha. Have you got hold of any recent pictures of Marty and Tracy?"

"Yep, got them from the PD file, and a few more from social media."

"Send me whatever you think are the best ones," Sam said. "I'm going to check some of the motels that are easiest to hide out in and see if I can find anyone who remembers either of them."

"Okay, Babe. I'll see what else I can find out."

"Try to find out all you can on these videos he does, okay? Especially the most recent ones, from the past three or four weeks. Marty disappeared almost two weeks ago, so I'm guessing he probably got into this trouble not long before that. If we can see what he was talking about, it might give us a better idea of what was going on."

"You got it," Indie said. "Love you!" The line went dead.

3

Sam went to more than a dozen motels scattered throughout the metro area, but didn't hit any pay dirt. He left the last one feeling frustrated and realized that it was getting close to lunchtime, so he headed for the house. Indie was just starting to make a lunch of ham and cheese sandwiches for herself, her mother and Kenzie, so she added another sandwich for Sam. He sat in the kitchen with her and told her what little he had learned.

"I wish you'd had better luck," Indie said. "Now, as for me and Herman, we did a little better, I think. I tracked down Marty's videos, and he does seem to have a lot to say." She picked up a tablet from the counter and handed it to Sam. "Just hit play," she said. "That's his last two videos."

Sam tapped the screen to wake up the tablet and saw that it was already on a YouTube app. There were two videos linked on the display, and he tapped the play icon on the first one.

Marty's face appeared, sitting behind the steering wheel of his van. His voice began to come though the speakers as the video finished buffering.

"Hey, it's Marty Fletcher again, and this time I'm gonna give you guys something I know is gonna get your *dander up!*" The last two words were said in a somewhat comical scream, and Sam's eyes went a bit wide. "I'm talking about the terrible drug problems in our streets, and how it never seems to get any better. Come on, you all know what I'm saying is true, right? You hear about all the big drug deals and busts, and it's a safe bet that pretty much everyone knows somebody who's been affected by what drugs can do to a person's life, right? So, how come, even though the USA has locked up more of its citizens than any other country on earth, and even though we have more cops and federal agents than any other country, the problem never seems to get smaller? If anything, it just gets bigger and bigger, year after year, and yet nobody wants to talk about why that is!"

A sudden camera cut made Marty's face jump closer to the camera, and his voice dropped to a stage whisper. "Well, I'm gonna tell you! This is one of the biggest secrets our government has, and I'm probably gonna make somebody mad, but it's got to come out. Are you ready?"

The scene jumped again, and Marty was back in his original position behind the wheel. "Here it is," he said. "It all goes back to prohibition, when it was against the law to make or sell alcohol in most of the country. The Department of Revenue, those federal agents that old movies refer to as 'revenooers,' were tasked with the job of finding out who was making or selling booze, and taking them to jail. But then, in 1933, prohibition was repealed, and all those revenooers were about to be out of a job. Congress couldn't have that black mark on their record, so they began enacting laws relating to the possession, use and sale of drugs, and all those federal agents began working on those laws. Sounds good so far, right?"

The scene jumped again, with Marty now sitting in the passenger seat. "*Wrong!*" he screamed. "What happened next was the realization that drugs meant lots and lots of money flowing through the country, and so the government began confiscating that money every time they made a bust! Millions and millions of dollars were confiscated every year, and a lot of that money never got accounted for. Instead, it went to the local offices of the agencies that confiscated it and was distributed *to the agents* as bonuses for doing the jobs they were supposed to be doing anyway!"

Back to the driver's seat. "So, why does the drug problem seem to keep going and going and going like that famous pink rabbit with the bass drum? That's simple! It's because there is just too much money involved, and since a lot of the people whose job it is to end the problem are actually benefiting financially from it, they're not about to work hard enough to kill their own personal golden goose!"

The video went on for several minutes, each scene cutting to a different view of Marty, until he ended it standing in front of the van and looking into the camera through the windshield. When Sam finally reached the end he looked up at Indie and shook his head. "He's a conspiracy nut," he said.

Indie nodded, then pointed at the tablet. "Watch the next one," she said.

Sam touched the play icon and the video began with a short commercial, then Marty's face appeared once again. This time, though, he was talking softly and his face appeared worried and frightened.

"Marty Fletcher here," he said, "and this may well be the last video I make. If you've been following me for any time at all, you know I don't pull any punches, but this time I've come up against something so bad I don't know how to handle it. When I get it figured out, gang, I promise you the most explosive video you've ever seen, and it's going to expose something so terrible that it may even lead to a federal investigation of the Denver Police! I can't say what it is just yet, but I will soon, so just keep watching this space, okay?" He started to reach toward the camera and then froze. "But if anything bad happens to me, then I'm sorry. I just can't post this up until I know how to handle certain aspects of it."

He reached up and apparently turned off the camera at that point, and Sam looked up at Indie.

"What in the world?"

She shrugged. "I don't know," she said. "That was his last upload from two weeks ago, and it's already gotten more than two hundred thousand views. The comments are filled with people demanding he post another one and reveal whatever he's learned, but there's been no response from him at all."

"Okay," Sam said after thinking for a moment. "I'm just not sure what to do, other than keep checking motels. I don't suppose you found anything on which motel the security footage came from, did you?"

"No, and that was kind of odd," Indie said. "There was mention that they had some footage showing Tracy and Marty going into motel rooms together going back several weeks, but none of the motels involved were named. Seems strange to me they'd be able to find so much in such a short time, unless maybe they were watching one or both of them before she disappeared?"

"Several weeks? What about the phone records? Have they been calling each other a lot?"

Indie shook her head. "Not until about two weeks ago. I scanned both of them, and there were occasional calls from Tracy's phone to Marty's, but none from his to hers. All of those were made during business hours, too, rather than in the evenings. Most people having affairs would have calls or text messages going both ways, wouldn't you think?"

"Good point. What about texts? Can you track those?"

"Yes, and while both of them text a lot, they never texted each other. That's another thing that seems off about the whole notion of them having an affair."

Sam nodded, and then the sandwiches were ready, so they tabled the conversation and called Kim and Kenzie in to eat. Sam got to hear about Kenzie's morning, with Kim spending time in the backyard playing with her granddaughter and the cat.

When lunch was over, Sam headed out again to keep checking motels. Indie had told him that Marty Fletcher drove a customized green Ford van, so Sam kept his eyes peeled for one like it as he drove from one motel to another throughout the afternoon, but once again he was having no luck.

Sam's phone rang at just before three, and he glanced at the screen to see that the call was from a blocked number. "Prichard," he said.

A gruff voice came on the line. "You the private dick who's looking for Marty Fletcher and his girlfriend?"

Sam's eyes grew wide. "I'm trying to locate Tracy Jensen," he said. "Who is this?"

"Well, this is Marty Fletcher, and we don't want to

be found," the voice said. "We'd appreciate it if you'd just leave us alone."

Sam scowled. "Really? I'd like to hear that from Tracy, then."

"She don't want to talk to you," the voice said. "She don't like to talk to nobody she don't know. She just wants you to leave us alone, okay?"

Sam whipped the Corvette to the curb and stopped. "Okay, listen, I just heard Marty's voice on a video, and you aren't him. And Tracy knows me quite well; we were engaged once, years ago, so if you're really with her, put her on the phone—"

The line went dead, and Sam growled in frustration. If he had needed anything to convince him Tracy really was in trouble, this ridiculous attempt to make him back off had done it. He sat there and thought for a moment, then called the Denver PD again.

"Jerry Lemmons, please," he said to the desk sergeant.

"Detective Lemmons."

"Jerry, it's Sam Prichard again. I know you said you don't think there's anything to the missing persons case, but I'm beginning to think differently. I've been looking into it, and someone just called me claiming to be Marty Fletcher and telling me to back off."

"Well?" Lemmons said. "Maybe the happy couple just wants to be left alone."

always says stuff like that to get women to like him.
They said it was the way he got them to leave their
families, but Mom isn't that stupid. She was really
scared for him, but she didn't want to be with him or
anything like that. She just didn't want him to get hurt,
y'know?"

Modus operandi, Sam thought. Get a woman to
worry about you, and you were halfway to seducing
her, or at least that was the way a lot of guys worked. If
Martin was that sort, it was quite possible Heather's
mother had fallen prey to it, after all.

"Heather, don't you think the police might know
something about this? From what I understand, your
mom wouldn't be the first woman he's tricked into
running away with him."

She shook her head. "Mom wouldn't," she said
emphatically. "The morning she disappeared, before
she went to work, she told me if anything happened to
her, if she got hurt or disappeared and no one would do
anything about it, I was supposed to come to you and
tell you that the cops are in on it and can't be trusted.
She said you'd know what to do."

That made both Sam's and Indie's eyebrows go
even higher. "She told you to come to me? How does
she know me?"

Heather looked at him shyly and cast a furtive
glance at Indie before turning back to Sam. "Because
she used to be your girlfriend," she said. "You were

11

"Come on, Jerry," Sam said with a growl. "I saw some of Fletcher's videos, and the voice on the phone didn't even sound a bit like him. He also told me Tracy wouldn't talk to me because she didn't know me, which tells me he doesn't know Tracy at all. If he did, he'd know that she's my ex-fiancé."

"Your ex-fiancé?" Lemmons asked. "Maybe she just never told him about you, you think of that?"

Sam rolled his eyes. "Thank you, Jerry," he said. "Assume Tracy ran off with this guy, and then somebody tells them that a private investigator named Sam Prichard is looking into her disappearance. Can you honestly tell me it wouldn't cross her mind to say, oh, crap, I know who that is? If nothing else, they would use that little detail to convince me the call was legitimate."

"I don't know what to tell you, Sam. We're dead certain the two of them ran off together. Maybe they got someone else to call you, and forgot to mention that little detail. Why don't you just let us handle this, okay? If you're just working for the kid, you're probably not getting paid anyway. Now, I'm sorry if I seem a little brusque, but I got a lot of work to do. I'll talk to you later, okay?"

Sam was holding a phone that was dead. He scowled at it for a couple of seconds, then shoved it back into his pocket.

Three lives to save, Sam thought. *Sure would be*

nice if I had some idea who they are!

4

The rest of the day was the same. Sam checked more than three-dozen motels that were commonly frequented by people who might not want to be noticed, but none of the desk clerks showed any sign of recognition when he handed them photos of Tracy or Marty. He finally gave it up at five and headed for home.

Kenzie was waiting at the door for him, the way she always was when she heard the loud pipes of the Corvette pulling into the driveway. "Daddy!"

Sam scooped her up into his arms for a hug, and then noticed both of her grandmothers sitting on the couch. They had Kenzie's entire assortment of Barbie dolls spread out between them, and his mother held one up and smiled. "Oh, look," she said in a voice that was pitched two octaves higher than her own, "Kenzie's daddy is home. Yay!"

"Yay," said Kim, holding up the Ken doll. "I was feeling all alone as the only boy in a house full of girls."

Sam couldn't help snickering. "It's great to be welcomed," he said.

Indie came out of the kitchen with a smile. "Hey, you're home," she said. "Any luck?"

Sam put Kenzie down and followed his wife back into the kitchen. As soon as they were alone, he pulled her into an embrace and kissed her quickly. "Nothing good," he said. "I did have one interesting moment, though. Some jackass called me up and claimed to be Marty Fletcher, then told me that he and Tracy were happy together and wanted me to back off. The only problem was that it wasn't Marty's voice, and this idiot wasn't aware that Tracy and I ever knew each other."

Indy's eyebrows shot up as she looked up at him. "Okay, that's weird," she said. "Did you get the number?"

Sam shook his head. "No, the caller ID was blocked. No idea who it could have been, but it definitely set off some alarm bells for me. I called Jerry Lemmons back and told him about it, thought maybe he'd agree that it sounded odd, but he says they're absolutely certain that Marty and Tracy are simply having an affair and have run off together."

Indy scrunched up her face. "Sam, that almost sounds like he knows something he's not telling," she said. "Can you think of any reason the police would be covering this up?"

"None that would make any sense. Just seems odd that somebody would try to throw me off the case, you know?"

Indy nodded. "Yeah. It makes Heather's insistence that her mom wouldn't run off willingly a lot more believable."

"It does more than that," Sam said. "It convinces me that Tracy must actually be in some kind of danger. There is something going on behind her disappearance, and it's something that somebody wants to keep secret. Maybe good old Marty really did stumble onto something big."

"So, where do you go from here? What's the next step?" Indie asked.

Sam shook his head as he sank into a chair at the table. "I'm not sure," he said. "What kind of magic can you work with that throwaway phone we think is Marty's? Isn't there some way you can figure out where it's at?"

"I could if I could get into the account behind it, but it's one of those cheap phones that just piggybacks on a major carrier. The carrier can't give me any information about whose account it is, so that means I can't get any of its electronic identification numbers. Without those, I can't get a GPS ping on it."

"What if I call the number? Can you get anything on

it if I get it on the line?"

Indy shook her head. "That doesn't really help. If it was actually on a major carrier, then I could identify the phone and trace its location, but the number it uses isn't really assigned to that particular device. It's like using a forwarding number—the carrier gives it a number to use, but then it's bounced through a switcher for whatever company sold it. Their equipment sends the call to that phone, but it's not sophisticated enough that I can follow it down to the device. That make sense?"

Sam grinned at her. "No, but I'm usually in the dark when you try to explain the technical stuff. I just hold onto my faith that you know what you're talking about and leave it at that." He rubbed a hand over his eyes and then looked back up at her. "Still, if I can get Marty on the phone, maybe I can get him to tell me what's going on. You got that number?"

Indy picked up the tablet that was lying beside Sam on the table and poked at its screen for a moment. "Here it is," she said as she handed it to him.

Sam took his phone out of his pocket and punched the number into its dial pad. It rang three times, and then Marty's voice answered.

"Hello?"

"Is this Marty? My name is Sam Prichard, I'm an old friend of Tracy's."

"You're the private eye, right? She mentioned you once."

"Right, that's right. I've been hired to try to locate Tracy, and I'm hoping you might be able to give me some idea where she is."

"Aw, crap," Marty said. "I was hoping she told you to call and tell me it was safe to come home. No, I'm sorry, I have no idea where she could be. I haven't heard from her in days, but the last time I talked to her she said something about asking you for help."

Sam's eyes narrowed. "When was that, Marty?"

"Would've been about three, maybe four days ago. She called and told me things were getting hot, and that she knew you and thought maybe you could help. She told me to stay out of sight and wait for her to call me again. I figured she must've given you this number, because as far as I know, she's the only one who had it."

"Actually, my wife is a computer whiz and she got it out of Tracy's phone records. Marty, are you aware that the police are claiming you and she ran off together?"

"Yeah, bullshit," Marty said. "They damn well know better than that. If Tracy's actually missing, you can bet your ass they know where she is, at least some of 'em."

"You think the police have something to do with her disappearance?"

"Hell, yeah," Marty said. "That's what this whole thing is about, man, dirty cops! I found out something

38

so bad they want me dead, and all Tracy was doing was trying to help me stay alive, y'know?"

A chill ran down Sam's spine. "Marty, what is it you know? Is it serious enough that Tracy might be in real danger?"

"Geez, man, we're all in danger! All I can tell you is we got some of the worst cops in the world, and you can't trust any of them!"

Sam thought for a moment. "Marty, I want to help you, and I want to find Tracy. Is there a place you and I can meet, to talk?"

Marty laughed, but there was no mirth in it. "Sorry, man, but I don't know for sure that you really are who you say you are. I'm not telling anybody where I'm at, you dig?"

"Yeah, I can understand," Sam said, "but I don't know how to help you. If you got something going on about corrupt cops, I can promise you I'll do whatever it takes to keep you safe and get them off your back. How about this? You pick a spot, anywhere you like, maybe someplace where you can watch from a distance and see that I really show up alone. I'll be driving a Corvette, it's easy to spot."

"No way, man, not gonna happen. I'm not meeting anybody right now. With Tracy gone, I have to figure I'm completely alone, I'm not sticking my neck out where it can get chopped off."

The phone went dead and Sam let out a sigh of

frustration. "He's not talking, so I'm back to square one."

"Okay," Indie said, "so what is square two?"

"Square number two is where I put this whole mess on the back burner until tomorrow morning, and just spend this evening with my family."

* * * * *

The following morning saw Sam checking more motels. He was getting discouraged after visiting so many, but since he had no other leads he kept going.

Sam pulled in at the Sunset Motel at a few minutes after ten and walked into its office. A young man of what looked to Sam to be Middle Eastern appearance smiled and spoke to him with no sign of an accent.

"Hi, there, need a room?"

Sam grinned and held out his ID. "No, thank you," he said. "My name is Sam Prichard, and I'm a private investigator."

"Pleased to meet you, Sir," the clerk said, holding out a hand to shake. "I'm Pete Patel."

Sam grinned and shook his hand. "Same here, Pete. Is that your real name?"

Pete put on a mock look of surprise. "Why, Sir, are you implying I don't look American enough to be named Pete?" He broke into a big smile and chuckled. "Actually, it really is my name. My parents came over here from India shortly before I was born, and I was named Peter after the man who sponsored them for citizenship."

Sam bowed his head slightly as an apology for his unintended stereotyping. "Pete, I'm looking for a woman who's gone missing, and I've heard she might have been seen at a motel around here last week." He took out his phone and called up the pictures Indie had sent him. He chose the photo of Tracy first, and held the phone out for the clerk to see. "Have you seen this woman coming and going?"

Pete looked at the photo for only a second, then smiled. "Yeah, that's her," he said. "She rented a room for her brother, or at least that's what she said. He had a green van that he kept hidden in the alley behind the motel." The smile became a conspiratorial grin. "I thought it was kind of strange the way she kept showing up and sneaking food into the room, and then there's the fact that her so-called brother never even stepped outside. The police have already been here asking about them, they even took our security tapes."

Sam nodded. "That figures. And you were right to think it was odd, since that wasn't her brother. I need to ask, though, is there anything else you might have noticed, something you might not have thought to tell the police? I'm trying to find this woman for her daughter. The police seem to think these two ran off together, but her daughter doesn't believe that."

The clerk looked into Sam's eyes for a moment,

41

then leaned a little closer and lowered his voice. "There was one thing," he said. "There was this one guy who came with her the day before the brother left. I was down in the room next door at the time, had to replace the ball valve in the toilet, and it sounded like they were all arguing. That made me curious, so I peeked out the window as she and the other man were leaving, and it looked to me like she was kinda scared of him. I didn't get a good look at the guy until they were getting into his car, but then I knew I'd seen him before so I started trying to remember where. It didn't hit me until later, but he's a cop." He turned and picked up a newspaper that was lying on the desk behind the counter and spun it around so Sam could see a photograph. The picture was attached to a very small story reporting Tracy's disappearance, and repeating the police theory that she had simply run away with a boyfriend. "That's the guy, right there."

Sam's eyebrows rose. The picture was a photograph of Detective Jerry Lemmons.

"This is the man who came with the woman and argued with the guy in the room?"

Pete nodded gravely. "That's him," he said. "Paper says he's the detective in charge of the case, and I thought that was a little weird. He didn't come by here himself to talk to me, he sent a couple of regular cops in uniform."

Sam looked into the young man's eyes for several

seconds. "And you didn't mention to those officers that you had seen this detective with her?"

"No, Sir," Pete said. "When they started asking questions like nobody knew anything about it, I got the funny feeling it might not be a good idea to admit I had seen that detective. He seemed pretty ticked off when he was here with that lady, and I didn't think I wanted him to get mad at me, if you know what I mean."

Sam nodded slowly. "I think that might've been a pretty smart decision on your part. I appreciate you telling me, and I promise you it'll stay between us."

Sam left the motel with more questions than he'd had when he arrived. Jerry Lemmons, a detective he'd known on the force for several years, could possibly be involved in Marty and Tracy's disappearance. Sam thought back to Heather's statement, saying that her mom had told her to come to Sam and tell him the police were involved and should not be trusted.

The problem was that Sam Prichard hated the thought of a crooked cop and would prefer to never have to deal with such a case, but he was also far too honest and stubborn to back down once it was dropped into his lap. If he became convinced Jerry Lemmons really was somehow involved in something criminal, Sam would do everything in his power to prove it and bring him to justice.

5

It was almost noon by the time he got back to his house and told Indie what he'd learned.

"How well do you know Lemmons?" Indie asked. "Would you have expected him to be involved in anything illegal?"

"We worked together in Vice a few times," Sam said, "but I can't say we were ever close. Would I expect this of him? I don't think I would expect it of any cop, but I'm also a realist and I know that it happens."

"I just wonder why Tracy would have taken him to see Marty," Indie said. "And then, of course, you have to wonder what the argument was about."

"And why Pete thought she looked scared when they were leaving. I can simply call him up and ask him, but somehow I suspect he'll deny it, and then I've got the problem of betraying Pete's confidence. I

44

promised I wouldn't let on that he told me about it."

"Right. So how do you plan to find out?"

Sam grinned. "Actually, I'm going to call on our old pal Herman and ask him to start digging into Jerry a little bit. Think he might be able to do that?"

Indie gave him a grin of her own. "I think I can talk him into it," she said. "But before we get to that, I've got some good news for you. Remember I told you I wouldn't be able to track down that phone Marty is using? Well, after you left this morning I started Herman scanning through every cheap phone provider, looking for that number."

"And he found something?" Sam asked, his eyebrows high.

"Yep. He got me the electronic serial number of the phone, which allowed me to ping its GPS location. That phone is sitting in Buckley Park in Montrose, over on the western side of the state."

"Montrose," Sam mused. "I know where that is. I'll let you dig into Jerry, and I'll head out to Montrose after lunch. If Marty is there, I intend to find him and get him to tell me exactly what's going on, and maybe that will help me figure out what happened to Tracy." He rubbed his eyes for a second. "If everything goes well, we might be able to clear this up pretty quick."

Indie looked at him for a moment. "Okay," she said. "As soon as we eat, I'll go pack your overnight bag. If you're gonna go that far, you might need to stay overnight somewhere."

Sam nodded. "Yeah, that thought occurred to me, too. You can check once in a while and see if that phone is moving, so maybe I can get right to it as soon as I get there. With any luck, I'll find Marty early enough that I can come back home tonight, but you never know."

Indie heated up a frozen pizza, and Sam joined his family at the table. Indie mentioned to Kenzie that Sam might need to be gone overnight, but the little girl was too excited to make a fuss. Both of her grandmothers were coming back over to play with her that afternoon, and she was busy planning Barbie's next adventure.

When lunch was finished, Indie shoved their plates into the dishwasher and Sam followed her to the bedroom. It only took a few minutes for her to put together his overnight bag, and then he took advantage of the bedroom door to get a few minutes of privacy with his wife. He wrapped his arms around her and pulled her close, and gave her a kiss that lasted more than a minute.

"That's just cruel," she said, after she caught her breath. "You kiss me like that just before you're leaving, all it does is leave me frustrated. If this guy Marty gives you any static when you get there, you tell him I'm going to beat his brains in for making you stay gone all night."

Sam grinned and kissed her again. "I'll be sure to

tell him that," he said. He stole one more quick kiss, then picked up his bag and went out to tell their daughter goodbye.

This time, Kenzie paid more attention. She ran to him and let him catch her up in a big hug, then kissed his cheek and made him promise to come home as soon as he could. "And, Daddy?"

"What, sweetheart?"

"Don't get shot again, okay?" The look in her eyes told her that she was genuinely worried for him, and almost brought tears to his own.

"I promise to do my best," he said. "Is that okay?"

Kenzie sighed. "I guess it'll have to do," she said, bringing grins to all three of the adult faces. Sam hugged her once more and put her down, then kissed Indie one more time before stepping out the door and climbing back into the Corvette.

The fastest route from Denver to Montrose was to take I-70 to Grand Junction, then head south on US 50. The trip would normally take almost five hours, but he ran into construction on the interstate just after passing Glenwood Springs, and it added another forty minutes.

Sam enjoyed driving, especially in the Corvette. He had plugged in a series of his favorite CDs; the music kept him alert and focused on the road. Occasionally, in between CDs, he would call home and talk to his wife and daughter for a few moments, but Sam preferred keeping his mind on the road.

By the time he pulled into Montrose, it was almost six thirty in the evening. He took out his phone and called Indie one more time as he passed the city limits sign.

"Any movement on the phone?"

"Just a moment," Indie said, "let me double check. No, right at the moment it's still showing up in Buckley Park, on Nevada Avenue."

"Okay," Sam said. "Does seem kind of strange that it hasn't moved at all, though. If Marty is hiding out here, you'd think he'd be going to one of these restaurants to eat now and then, right?"

"Yeah, but maybe he leaves the phone in his van. If Montrose is like a lot of the small towns around Colorado, you can camp in the parks. Maybe he keeps the phone plugged in to keep the battery up."

Sam grinned into the phone. "That's one of the things I love about you," he said. "You always tend to look on the brighter side of things. Me, I wonder if the fact the phone isn't moving around might indicate that Marty isn't capable of it. Hang on a second, I see a sign for the park. Let me take a look real quick while I've got you on the phone."

Sam turned onto North Fourth Street and followed it two blocks up to the park. There were several vehicles scattered around the area, and it took him only a moment to spot the green and silver Ford van.

"Indie, I think I see his van. I'm gonna park a little

ways off and try to stroll up there quietly without being seen. I'll call you back when I know something."

"You'd better," Indie said. "Good luck, Babe." She hung up without another word and Sam slipped his phone into his pocket as he parked the Corvette alongside the park on the street.

He stepped out of the car and felt his hip twinge, so he reached back inside to grab his cane. He usually didn't need it much anymore, but sitting for so long in the bucket seat was enough to cause the hip to hurt when he started to put his weight on it. He leaned lightly on the cane, just enough to take a little pressure off the once badly damaged joint.

He had parked about fifty yards from the van, leaving the Corvette out of sight from anyone who might be inside it. He strolled along leisurely, as if he was merely enjoying the afternoon, meandering along the way so that it would not be obvious that he was trying to get a look through the windshield. He passed about 10 feet in front of the van and quickly turned his head toward it as he did so.

The interior was dark and Sam couldn't tell if anyone was inside the van or not, so he continued walking for another moment. He stopped and leaned against a tree, then slowly turned himself around so that he could see the van again.

It rocked just a bit as he was watching it, but its darkened windows made it impossible to see any motion inside. Still, someone was moving around inside there, probably trying to keep an eye on him. He pushed off from the tree and started walking directly toward the vehicle.

It rocked again as the occupant moved to watch him through another window, so Sam stepped up his pace. 15 seconds later he was standing just beside the driver's door, and he knocked softly on the window.

"Martin Fletcher?" he asked. "I'm Sam Prichard, we talked on the phone a while ago."

There was silence from inside the van for half a minute, and then it moved again as a man inside climbed up into the driver's seat. It took Sam a moment to realize that it was Marty, because his normally black hair had been dyed blonde and he was sporting a pair of horn-rimmed glasses. He looked at Sam for a couple of seconds, then the window rolled down about three inches.

"You're the private detective?" Marty asked.

"I am," he said as he flashed his ID. "And I'm in no mood to play games. Let me in so we can talk privately."

Marty looked at him for another moment, then pointed toward the passenger side. "Okay," he said. "Climb in. I don't want anyone to overhear us."

Sam nodded, then walked around the front of the van and reached for the passenger door. There was a click, and then the lock button popped up. Sam opened the door and climbed up inside, shutting it behind him.

"How did you find me?" Marty asked. "I didn't think anyone knew I was here."

"It was actually pretty easy," Sam replied. "We got into Tracy's cell phone records and realized that when she stopped calling your phone every day, she started calling another one. Once we had that number, it was just a matter of time before we were able to get your GPS location. Now tell me, do you have any idea where Tracy might be? Her daughter is pretty worried about her."

Marty frowned and shook his head. "Ain't got a clue," he said. "She told me to come out here while she tried to work some kind of magic, but I haven't heard from her in a couple of days now. The last time she called me was two, no, three days ago. She said she was thinking about trying to get hold of you, and seeing if you could get it all fixed so I could come home, but not to leave where I was at until I heard from her. When you called earlier, I was hoping she was having you call to tell me everything's okay."

"I'm afraid not," Sam said. "She didn't come home from work the day you last talked to her, but the police seem to think you and she ran off together."

Marty snorted, a derisive laugh. "Like heck they do," he said. "Tracy brought this cop out to see me last week, a detective named Lemmons. I guarantee you, he knows exactly what's going on. If Tracy is missing, I'd bet money he knows where she is."

"I know Detective Lemmons," Sam said. "He's actually the one in charge of the non-existent investigation into Tracy's whereabouts, and he's the one who insists that you two were having an affair and ran off together. Care to enlighten me about why he would say that?"

"Because he's scared," Marty said. "He knows what this is all about, and it scares the crap out of him."

Sam raised an eyebrow. "And just exactly what is it all about? What's going on that would scare a police detective?"

Marty looked at him for a moment, then turned his attention to the steering wheel, where his fingers were picking at the horn button. He was silent for a few seconds, then turned back to Sam.

"Look, I know Tracy said we could trust you, but we're talking about my life, here. I'm not sure how much I really want to tell you at this point, can you dig it? You may be the stand-up guy she thinks you are, but money and threats can make people do some pretty weird stuff."

Sam shook his head in confusion. "Money and threats? Where does that come in?"

Marty gave him a sarcastic grin. "Let's just say certain people are probably willing to pay a lot, or do just about anything, to get their hands on something I've got. That would include killing me and anyone else who knows too much about it."

Sam leaned against the passenger door. "Marty, I'm here to try to help you, because right now you're the only lead I've got on finding Tracy. The trouble is, I can't help either of you if you keep stalling me. Just what is it you've got hidden away, and why is it so important?"

Marty stared at him for several seconds before he answered. "Okay, fine," he said, "but just remember I warned you, this isn't something you even want to get involved in. And if you're thinking about trying to collect some reward, you can forget it right now. They might promise to pay a lot, but all you'd end up getting is a bullet in the head. They can't take a chance you might talk about it afterward."

"I'm not interested in any reward," Sam said. "If Tracy told you anything at all about me, then you probably know she was once very important to me. I'm here for her, not for any money. Whatever you tell me will stay between us for as long as it needs to. I'm just hoping it'll give me some kind of lead on how to find Tracy and keep her safe."

"I think she's safe enough at the moment. They won't risk hurting her as long as they don't have it, and she doesn't know where it is." He stared another moment and then sighed. "Okay, I'll tell you. It's a video recording," he said. "And what makes it so valuable is that it shows five cops, including your pal

Lemmons, murdering three kids."

6

Sam's eyes were about to fly out of his head. "Murdering *kids*?" he asked incredulously.

Marty shrugged. "Two boys and a girl, not one of them over sixteen. And now you're gonna tell me there's no way you believe it, right?"

Sam got his eyes back under control and stared at the other man. "No," he said slowly. "No, I'm not going to say that outright, because I know how bad people can be. What I am going to say is that I'd certainly like to get a look at that video, but more important than that, I want to know how and why it happened. Can you tell me that?"

"I can tell you the how pretty easily, since I saw it all on the video," Marty replied. "They beat the boys to death with their bare hands, but the girl was strangled. She was screaming, so one of them just wrapped his arm around her throat and started squeezing until she went limp, but then he just stood there and held on for another couple of minutes, staring at the others and what they were doing to those boys. A cop held one of the boys while Lemmons pounded on his face 'til there was almost nothing left, and the other boy got the same treatment, with one holding him while the other one beat on him." He swallowed, and Sam could see the disgust in his face. "As for the why, I think it was just for the thrill of it. One of the boys got mouthy with a couple of the cops, and Lemmons punched him. He said they were gonna learn a lesson, but when they realized the girl was dead, they started to freak. Lemmons said they couldn't let anyone find out what happened, so the cops choked the boys until they were dead, too."

Sam shook his head in shock. "Good Lord," he said. "What on earth started it all?"

"The kids were caught somewhere they shouldn't have been, by two uniform cops. At first it just looked like they were gonna get chewed out and sent on their way, but then one boy started running his mouth, saying the cops didn't have any right to tell him what to do, and how all cops ought to be shot, and one of them hit him in the face. The other boy tried to fight, jumping on the cop that punched his friend, so the other cop called for backup and grabbed that one and the girl, then they just stayed there until another squad car and that asshole Lemmons showed up. They asked the kids what was going on and one of them said the cops just attacked them for no reason, but then Lemmons started slapping that boy around. One of the first pair of cops was holding onto that kid, and the new ones started on the second boy while the other one was holding the girl. That was when the girl started to scream and it all went crazy. Lemmons said to shut her up, and next thing they knew, she was dead. After that, it looked like they all just decided the boys had to die to cover their own asses."

Sam was staring at him. "How long ago did this happen? I haven't heard anything about dead teenagers lately..."

"What about missing teenagers? On the video, you can see them loading the kids' bodies into the trunk of one of the cars, and then they all drove away together. My guess is they took 'em somewhere they won't be found any time soon, wouldn't you think?""

Sam thought about it for a moment, and then nodded slowly. "Couple of weeks ago, right? There was a story on the news about a teenage girl going missing, and her family thought she might have run off with a couple of boys she'd been hanging out with. News reports said the boys were missing, too, but they'd been known to disappear from time to time so no one was really worried about them. If the girl hadn't been known as a pretty good kid from a money family, it probably would have gone unnoticed for a while."

"I'd say that was probably them," Marty said softly. "Timing's about right."

Sam looked at him. "And how is it that you have a video of all this?"

"I didn't know I did until the next day," Marty sighed. "I keep a camera in my van for these videos I do, a video blog thing. That evening, I made a new one down on Vine Street, in a parking lot, and then a buddy of mine called me and wanted me to go have a few beers with him, so I locked up the van right there and he came and picked me up." He shrugged. "Thing is, I forgot to shut off the camera. It was pointed out the windshield from when I'd made my last vid, and I just didn't notice the little light was still flashing, so I just forgot about it, right? When I got back to it about three that morning, I went home and took it in so I could download the video into my computer and edit it. That went fine and I uploaded it to YouTube, then went to bed. The next day, I noticed I still had several hours of video left in the download, and I don't even know why, but I scanned through it at high speed, and that's when I saw cops. I slowed it down and watched, and then I pretty much crapped myself. That's a top-quality camera with a terabyte of storage and a super-sensitive microphone, and it caught the whole thing, audio and all. I trimmed out all the dead time, uploaded it to a private server nobody even knows I've got, then started wondering what the heck to do about it."

He fell silent, so Sam asked, "And what did you decide?"

Marty shrugged again. "I didn't know what to do. Couldn't go to the cops, right? Everyone knows they cover for each other, so that would only get me killed. Couldn't just broadcast it on YouTube, it would get shut down within minutes and no one would ever believe anyone who said they saw it. I thought about emailing a link to the news people on TV, but I don't trust them anymore than I trust cops, so that was out. I've been trying to figure out how to use it to make those suckers pay for what they did, but I just don't have any ideas that won't get me killed."

"I can help with that," Sam said. "I can get it to the people who'll prosecute the officers involved, trust me. The question for this moment, though, is where is Tracy? How did she get involved in all this?"

Marty grinned sadly. "Tracy's a great gal," he said. "We work together, y'know, and she cornered me in the racks a day or so after all that and said she could tell something was eating at me. I tried to brush it off, but she wouldn't let me, so that evening after work, we went out for a bite to eat and I ended up spilling it all." He sighed and the grin faded away. "She was shocked at first, of course, couldn't believe I was telling the truth, so I used my phone to show her the part where they realized the girl was dead and she freaked. When she calmed down, she started talking about how the girl didn't look any older than her daughter, and said she wanted to help me out. She even mentioned trying to get you to help us, but I was so scared I didn't want to trust anyone, so she tried to talk me into letting her take it to the news or some such, but that scared me, too. We decided to just think about it for a couple days, and then I got a message on YouTube that said someone saw my van in that parking lot that night, and wanted to talk to me about anything I might've seen."

"Did you reply?"

Marty nodded, his eyes closed. "Yeah," he said. "I thought maybe it was someone else who'd seen it, and wanted me to back up their story, y'know? And sure as hell, he wanted to know if I had seen some cops doing something really bad that night. I told him I didn't see it myself, but I'd got it on video, and that's when he said it was worth a lot of money. He said he knew how to sell it to the news people, like CNN or somebody, and wanted me to give it to him. That's when I started to get nervous about it, though, cause when I said I'd give him a copy, he got all pissed off. He said he could only sell it if he had the only existing copy, which is BS, and I stopped talking to him."

"What happened then?"

"Couple of cops showed up at my work the next morning. I was late coming in and saw the squad car sitting there, so I went on by and called Tracy on her cell. She said they were asking about me, and I panicked. I went and hid in a buddy's garage all that day, and that night Tracy got me a motel room to stay in while she tried to get hold of someone to help me. I was willing to do anything by that point, so when she told me she knew a cop who said he was willing to help, I told her it was okay to bring him over. I just about died when I saw who it was."

"Jerry Lemmons," Sam said flatly. "Any idea how she got involved with him on this?"

Nodding, Marty said, "Yeah. She knew him, but she didn't recognize him on the video, cause the screen on my phone was so small, and I think she was freaked out about the girl, anyway. I guess she'd dated him once, back before she married her husband, but she remembered him while all this was going on and called him up. When she told him what it was about, I guess he made all the right noises. She brought him to the motel, and when I panicked and said he was one of the cops on the video, he pulled out a gun and said he'd shoot her if I didn't hand it over. I told him I didn't have it with me, and that it was in a place where it would be found by someone who'd do something about it if anything happened to me or Tracy." He sighed deeply. "But then he stopped that gun against her head, so I promised to have it delivered to him if he'd promise not to hurt us. He said he'd give me twenty-four hours, and later that night Tracy called and told me to run. I said I couldn't leave her stuck in it all by herself, and that's when she said she had a plan, but if Lemmons got his hands on me it would all fall apart. I jumped in my van and came out here, and the last time I talked to her was when she said she was going to try to talk to you and would call me back. Never heard anything from her again, but the next night I saw she'd called while I was out scrounging some food. I tried calling her back, but it went straight to voicemail."

Sam thought over all he'd heard for a moment, then looked at Marty again. "You think Lemmons has her somewhere? Or do you think she's dead?"

Marty shook his head emphatically. "She's not dead," he said. "Lemmons isn't that stupid. I think he knows the only thing keeping me from spreading this all over creation right now is knowing he'd kill her if I do. I think he's got her stashed somewhere, and he's hoping he can use her to find me and get that video, but I never told her where I was."

Sam nodded slowly. "I think you're right. He'll keep her alive until he's got his hands on the recording, I agree. Can you show me this video? I want to see it."

Marty looked at him for a long moment, then reached down under the seat and came up with a tablet. He held it so Sam couldn't see it, tapped on the screen for a few seconds, then handed it over. "Just tap the arrow."

Sam stared at the screen for a moment, then tapped the video play icon.

7

This video had not been edited, and Sam was amazed that chance had caused the camera to be facing precisely the right direction to capture the entire sequence of events. It opened suddenly, showing three young people walking into view in an alleyway. There were two boys, one of whom was black, and a girl. The other boy and the girl appeared to be Caucasian. Sam realized he was looking into the alley from a spot in a parking lot that abutted it. A lamp above the building illuminated the scene.

A police cruiser appeared in the alley, its lights flashing once as it stopped, facing the three young people. Two officers stepped out of it, and Sam heard one of them say, "Just stop right there. What are you doing back here, this time of night?"

The white boy, now visible in the light, flipped a finger up. "Screw off, pig, we ain't doin' nothin'!"

The officer who had spoken looked at his partner. "Pig?" he asked. "Did he just call me a pig?"

"Sure sounded like it," the second officer said.

The first officer turned back to the boy and took a step forward. "What's your name, kid?"

The boy fluffed up like a cat facing a dog. "I ain't telling you, pig, what you think about that? You ain't got no business hangin' us up, we just walkin' through here is all. Go find a donut shop, why don't you?"

The two officers glanced at one another, then the first one spoke again. "Look, punk, I don't have to take this crap from you. Just tell us who you are, okay, before we start thinking you three are behind all the burglaries around here lately. Give us your names and then go home."

"Man, who you think you are, tellin' me to go home? You ain't shit, pig! You just like all them cops gettin' shot nowadays, just a target in your flashy blue suit, and it's about time people wise up and start blowin' your asses away! Every time I hear about another cop gettin' killed, I just think, yeah, that's it! Kill 'em all!"

It happened so fast that even Sam didn't see it coming. The cop who'd been speaking reached out and slapped the boy across the face so hard that he fell to the ground, and then the black boy jumped on him, punching him once in the mouth before he could react. Sam saw the second officer speak into the microphone on his shoulder, then reach out and grab the boy who'd struck his partner while holding onto the girl by an arm. The first officer had subdued the other boy on the ground, and placed cuffs on his wrists.

The two on their feet were muttering, but Sam couldn't hear what was being said. The second officer told them both to shut up, then looked at his partner. "Slocum, we taking these kids in?"

Slocum, the first cop, got to his feet and dragged the handcuffed boy up beside him. "Wait 'til backup gets here," he said. "I don't know if it's worth messing with it." He looked at the boy he was holding onto. "So, what were you doing here? Waiting for someone to bring you something?"

The kid spat onto the ground. "Screw you," he said. "We weren't doin' nothin'! You pigs just like to pick on anyone you can."

A second squad car came into view and parked beside the first one. Two officers stepped out, and Sam recognized one of them as David Forsyth. Forsyth had worked with him for a short time when he was with Vice, but had decided to return to uniform patrol after his wife complained about the job he was doing.

Forsyth walked over to where Slocum was still holding the boy he'd cuffed. "What've we got here?" he asked.

"Got some punks who think the police can't touch 'em," Slocum said. "This one thinks we all oughta be shot, and his pal over there took a swing at me when I shut this one's mouth for him."

The black boy tried to yank free of the officer holding him. "Hey, he attacked Kevin for no reason," he yelled. "You cops can't just punch somebody when you feel like it, there was no reason to hit any of us!"

"Shut up," Forsyth said. He turned to the boy who'd been named as Kevin. "Kevin what? What's your last name?"

"Screw you," Kevin said.

Forsyth turned at the sound of another car door that was out of sight of the camera and grinned. "What are you doing out this time of night?"

Jerry Lemmons came into view. "I was heading home from doing a scene report," he said, "and heard the call for backup. What's going on here?"

Slocum shook the boy he was holding. "Found some delinquents loitering in the alley, and asked them what they were doing here..."

The boy tried to yank away. "That's bull," he said. "We were just minding our own business and these two jackboots came up and started smackin' us around! You think just because you got badges means you like God, or somethin', you can do anything you want. That ain't how it is, pig, and people gettin' sick of it. That's why all you mothers keep gettin' shot, and I laugh every time I hear about it."

Lemmons looked around at the other officers and

then turned back to the kid. "Sounds to me like these punks need to learn a little respect for the law, don't it?" The other officers nodded, and Lemmons instantly punched the boy in the mouth.

The other boy yelled something Sam couldn't make out, but Lemmons struck again. "That one needs a lesson, too," he said, and Slocum grabbed the black boy from behind by both arms. Forsyth's partner immediately stepped up and punched the kid, and that's when the girl began to scream.

"You punks think you're pretty cool, right?" Lemmons asked. "You run around with this little tramp, she's kinda hot, right? Make you feel like big men? Well, now she's got you in some trouble you can't get out of. We're gonna make you wish you'd never seen her before."

The punching and screaming went on for several seconds, but then Lemmons stopped and looked at the girl. "Driscoll, you want to shut her up?" he asked, and Sam's wide eyes watched in horror as Officer Driscoll yanked the girl backward and tightened his arm around her throat. She reached up with both hands to try to pull the arm away, but it was obvious that she was having trouble breathing.

Lemmons and the other cop went back to punching their respective victims, while Driscoll held onto the girl and stared at what they were doing. The look on his face, Sam thought, would probably make a fitting illustration of sadistic glee. The girl struggled in his grip for only a few seconds, but then Sam saw her attempts grow more feeble until they finally stopped altogether. Her arms dropped to her sides and her face went slack.

Even knowing what he was seeing, Sam kept hoping that Driscoll would realize what was happening and release the girl, but it didn't happen. As the two boys began to sag in the arms of the cops holding them, Lemmons glanced over at Driscoll and realized that something was wrong.

"God, Driscoll," he shouted, "don't choke her to death!" Driscoll released the pressure on the girl's throat, but when he did she simply slid down him to the ground. He knelt down and felt for a pulse on her throat, then looked up at Lemmons with a face transformed into shock.

"Oh, geez," he said. "Geez, Jerry, I think she's dead."

Lemmons took only a few seconds to take stock of the situation. He stared at the girl, then at Driscoll, then looked at the other policemen. "Well, hell," he said. "This comes out, we're all jacked."

Forsyth appeared to be in shock, himself. He reached for the microphone on his shoulder, but Lemmons grabbed his hand before he could activate it. "What the hell?" Forsyth demanded. "We need to call for an ambulance, maybe it's not too late, maybe…"

Slocum was staring at his partner. "Oh, Jesus," he said. "They'll hang us all! What the hell are we gonna do?"

The other cops looked from one to another, then all of them turned toward Lemmons. They simply stared at him for a moment, until he nodded his head.

"We finish this," he said. The others stared at him for a moment, then Lemmons and Forsyth's partner put their hands around the boys' throats. Forsyth only stood there, his mouth agape.

It was over in a matter of minutes, as both boys went limp and breathed their last. When it was all over, Lemmons motioned toward Slocum. "Got anything in your trunk we can use to wrap them up?" he asked coldly. "Last thing we need is any of their blood showing up inside a car."

Slocum stared at him for a few seconds longer, then jogged over to the car and opened the trunk. He came back a moment later with an orange tarpaulin, and Lemmons helped him spread it out on the ground. They laid the three kids' bodies on it, and then Lemmons and the cop who'd strangled the other boy wiped their hands off on the girl's clothing. Seconds later, the four uniform officers picked up the unwieldy bundle and carried it to the trunk of the squad car.

The camera couldn't quite see what was going on, but the faint sounds made it obvious they were pushing and shoving the bodies inside. Lemmons had followed them back behind the car, and while Sam could hear him speaking, he couldn't make out the words.

Slocum and his partner got into the car and started it up, while the other two officers climbed into their own. Both cars drove away, leaving Lemmons alone at the scene. He pulled a small flashlight out of a pocket and shined it down on the ground, examining the scene for any signs of what had happened there. He kicked dirt over what must have been spatters of blood, then turned and started toward where he had left his car. For a brief moment, he glanced directly at the camera and seemed to stare at it for just a couple of seconds, but then he passed out of view.

The video ended, and Sam stared at the blank screen for several seconds before turning his gaze back to Marty.

"Lemmons is bad enough," he said, "but you're not just dealing with him. There are five city cops on that video, and any one of them would want you dead. I'm sure Lemmons has got them working with him, and I don't even know who one of them is. If this gets out before we find Tracy, I expect at least one or two of them would disappear in a hurry, and we'd probably never find her at all."

Marty nodded. "That's why I haven't even tried to do anything with it. It's bad enough those kids are dead, but how many more will they kill to cover it up? I mean, my folks still live in Littleton, and there's always

Tracy's husband and daughter. Sooner or later, they're going to start thinking about who else they could use against me, so I figured the best thing I could do is make sure they can't reach me. A threat like that wouldn't help if they don't know how to get it to me, right?"

Sam looked at him for a moment, then slowly turned his head and scanned the park around them. "The trouble with that is, if I could find you this easily then so can they. In fact, I'm kind of wondering why they haven't done anything about you yet."

8

Marty looked around nervously. "Geez, you think they're watching me now?"

Sam shrugged. "I don't see any sign of it, but it's possible. They have access to the same phone records I used to find you, though it's possible they might not have realized the strange number these last few days must have gone to you. Sooner or later, they will, and you don't want to be where they can find you if that happens."

Sam took a pen and a small notepad out of his pocket and scribbled something down. He tore off the page and passed it to Marty, who glanced at it.

I'm driving the Corvette. Follow me when I leave, but toss that phone out here. I'll take you to my dad's old hunting cabin. You'll hide there while I figure out what to do about this. Don't say anything about this out loud. Possible to listen in on phone even when off. I'm trying to keep you safe.

Marty read through the note quickly, then looked up at Sam. He nodded without saying a word, then took the phone out of his pocket and tossed it out the window.

Sam stepped out of the van and walked directly to the Corvette, leaning on his cane as his hip gave him trouble. He heard the van start behind him as he approached the car, then climbed in and fired it up. He pushed in the clutch and put the car in gear, then glanced toward the van as he began to pull away. He nodded once to himself as the van pulled out and moved to fall in behind him.

As soon as they were out of town, Sam took out his phone and called his wife. "Hey, Babe," he said when she answered. "I found him, right where you said he would be."

"Okay," she said. "Did he have any idea what might have happened to Tracy?"

"He's told me what he knows," Sam said. "I now have a pretty good idea what's going on and who might be behind her disappearance. Has Herman come up with anything on Jerry?"

"Nothing special," Indie said. "He tends to spend a lot of time at the casinos in Black Hawk, and he's been reprimanded twice this year for excessive use of force. Is there anything in particular I should be looking for?"

"Just anything that might be generally suspicious. I'm not going to go into it over the phone, but there's something truly horrible involved in all this, and he has plenty of reason to want it kept quiet."

Indie frowned, and Sam could hear it in her voice. "Sam, should I be worried?"

"I don't think so, not at this point at any rate. I doubt he knows that I'm on to any of this just yet. If he does, then you can definitely be worried about your hubby, but I think I can handle myself. I'm more concerned about the things your mom said. Marty and Tracy would be two of the lives I need to save, but I don't have a lead on the third one yet."

"Unless it's your own."

"I'll confess that could be a possibility," Sam said, "and now that I think of it, I've changed my mind. I want you to take Kenzie and go somewhere safe. It's probably not going to be long before Jerry knows I'm involved in this, and that could make you both targets. Take the grandmas with you, too." Sam chewed on his bottom lip for a moment. "Indie, how likely is it that the police can trace a phone as easily as you can?"

"How likely? They could probably do it even faster than Herman. Frankly, I'm surprised they hadn't already found Marty. The only thing I can figure is that they didn't realize the new number on Tracy's list of calls had to be going to him."

"Let's think about this for a moment," Sam said. "They had Tracy's phone logs, because that's where you got them, right? That means they could see everything you could, so what would be the chance they would miss a clue that big?"

"I grant you, that does seem kind of odd," Indie said. "But if they saw it, and really wanted to get to him, how on earth could you have gotten to him first? They would have either already had him, or someone would have been watching him when you got there."

Sam worried his bottom lip again. "Indie, get off the phone and get out of there, now. Leave your phone at home, leave all the phones at home, and get out of town. Get yourself a throwaway and call me once you've gotten somewhere safe. And don't forget, I love you. Kiss Kenzie for me. Get moving, now."

"We love you too," Indie said and the line went dead.

Sam put the phone back in his pocket, then concentrated on his driving, heading north on Route 50 again. His mind was racing, trying to decide just how to handle the situation he had found himself in.

Marty stayed on his tail as he drove. They made it as far as Glenwood, and then Marty begin flashing his lights. Sam took the hint and pulled in at the next gas station.

"Sorry about this," Marty said. "I wasn't expecting to take a trip today, so it didn't occur to me to gas up."

"Don't worry about it," Sam replied. "I could stand to top off myself." He slid a card into the reader on the gas pump, then opened his gas cap and pushed the nozzle inside. He squeezed the handle to start the gas flowing, then looked back at Marty. "You got gas money?"

"Yeah, I got it." Like Sam, he used a card to start the gas flowing. "So, this place we're going. Nobody else knows about it?"

"Nobody outside my family. You'll be safe there. The only neighbors are deer and rabbits, and I don't think they're going to bother you very much."

"Do I need to pick up any supplies?"

"Might be a good idea," Sam said. He glanced around at the store that was the office of the gas station. "We can probably get most of what you might need here. I think, once we get there, you might want to just stay put and keep that van out of sight."

"That sounds like a plan to me," Marty said. "I can get by with ramen noodles and canned spaghetti for a while, as long as I've got coffee and sugar."

They finished pumping their gas and went into the store. Marty gathered up several days' worth of food and snacks, then took it all to the register. A bored clerk checked him out and stuffed it all into bags. Five minutes later, they were back on the road.

They were almost to the exit they would have to take to get to the cabin when Sam's phone rang. He didn't recognize the number, so he answered cautiously. "Prichard," he said.

"It's me," Indie said. "We're going to..."

"Don't tell me," Sam said quickly. "Jerry could have my number tapped by now, and I don't want anyone to know where you are. Have you got the GPS turned off on that phone?"

"First thing I did. I'm also bouncing it through a couple of VoIP servers, something even Herman would have trouble tracing. Nobody can get a location on me, I promise."

Sam smiled into the phone. "That's my girl," he said. "Let's keep it that way. This thing is bad enough that there's no doubt in my mind Jerry would try to use you against me if he got the chance."

"Can you tell me now what's going on? This is scaring me, Sam."

"I'll give you the short version. Marty is in possession of a video showing Jerry Lemmons and four other cops committing murder. The victims were three teenagers, and one of them is the girl who went missing a couple weeks back. I don't have all the details yet, but somehow they found out the video exists and they want it pretty badly. Tracy got involved just to try to help Marty out, but when she went to a cop she knew for help, it turns out it was Lemmons himself. My guess is they've got Tracy stashed away somewhere, hoping to use her as leverage against Marty, to make him surrender the video."

"But if he does, then he and Tracy are both dead. Right?"

"No doubt about it," Sam said. "That video is the only reason they're both probably alive right now, and Marty was smart enough to have a copy stashed somewhere that they can't get to even if they kill him. He was supposed to surrender it a few days ago, but Tracy told him to run and hide. That would have been the day she disappeared."

"And with Lemmons running the investigation, it's easy for him to keep saying that the two of them just ran away together. Heather was right, but no one is going to believe a fourteen-year-old girl."

"Exactly, and that's what Lemmons is counting on. He's the investigating detective, so his word will be final on it until the truth comes to light. I'm stashing Marty in the safest place I can think of, and then Lemmons and I are going to have a little talk. I hope to convince him that the copy I've got is the only one, get him to give up Tracy in exchange for it. Once I've got her out and safe, then I'll deal with exposing the truth."

"Oh, Sam," Indie said, "you just be careful. Murderers are bad enough, but cops who murder are far more dangerous than anyone else."

"Think I don't know that? Trust me, babe, I don't plan to give them a chance at me. As long as I know you're safe, there isn't much they can use against me. You just stay put, and I'll call you when I know something more."'"

"Okay, baby. Stay safe." The line went dead again.

Sam turned off on the exit a few moments later, with Marty right on his tail. The smaller roads that led to his father's old cabin slowed them down a bit, and Sam was able to watch the road behind them in the mirror. He saw no signs they were being followed, and begin to relax just a bit.

Forty-five minutes later, Sam winced as the bottom of the Corvette dragged over occasional rocks in the rutted gravel road that led to the cabin. Because it was in such bad shape, he was forced to move at a snail's pace. When he finally got to the cabin and parked in its driveway, he breathed a sigh of relief that the mufflers still seemed to be intact.

Marty parked beside him and Sam let him inside, pulling the string that turned on the single electric light bulb in the combined living room and kitchen. The cabin was a little dusty, since no one had been there in almost a year, but at least it was solid and safe from the elements. Marty carried in the bags of groceries and snacks, setting them on the old wooden table in the kitchen area.

He stared at the old hand pump over the kitchen sink. "Rustic," he said. "I don't suppose there's any hot water for a shower?"

Sam grinned at him. "I'm afraid not," he said. He opened a cabinet, then pulled out a large kettle and set it on the counter beside the sink. "Fill that up from the pump and heat it on the stove. There's a big washtub, almost as big as a bathtub, on the back porch. By the time you heat up a couple of kettles of water and add some cold water to get the temperature where you want it, you can take a pretty nice bath. There's a bedroom through that door, and two more up in the loft."

Marty rolled his eyes but didn't make any comments. Sam showed him around the rest of the cabin and got him settled in.

"I want you to stay here and keep out of sight until I come for you," Sam said. "Now that you're hidden away, I'm going to try to convince Lemmons that you hired me to negotiate the surrender of the video. I'll offer to trade it for Tracy, and once she and her family are also safe, then we'll get it to the people who will actually take action on it. There's nothing I hate more than a dirty cop, and these bastards are going down."

"Okay," Marty said. "What makes you think he'll go along with it?"

"Simple," Sam said. "I need a copy of the video to show him. If I can convince him it's the only copy, then there's a chance this will actually work."

Marty shook his head. "No way," he said. "I told you, the only copy that exists right now is on a secret server on the Internet, and I'm the only one who knows the link. You might be a great guy and all, but if I give up that link I'm a dead man."

"I don't need your link," Sam said. "I just need you to put a copy of it on my phone. You can do that, can't you?"

Marty chewed his bottom lip for a moment, then nodded. "I've got a better idea," he said. He picked up his tablet and poked at the screen for a couple of minutes, then handed it over to Sam.

"You got lousy cell signal out here," he said, "but I managed it. I downloaded a copy onto the tablet, but I've encrypted it so that it can't be copied or shared. If you try to copy it off or email it to somebody else, it won't work. You show him that and he might believe it's the only copy."

"Brilliant," Sam said with a smile. "Listen, I don't have any way to reach you except to come up here," he said. "I'll make this happen as fast as I can, but you've got to stay here out of sight. Don't go into town, don't go driving around. This is the only place I can think of where Lemmons won't be able to find you."

"Don't worry," Marty said. "I think the last thing I want to do is leave this spot right now."

"Good. Just stay put. There's a lot of books here, so it might be a good time to just catch up on your reading. There is no TV, and no internet, so that's about all you've got."

"Trust me, I'll be fine. Reading actually sounds like a good way to pass the time."

Sam promised to get back to him as soon as possible, then left him in the cabin and started the long, slow drive back down the mountain. Miraculously, the mufflers survived, and Sam made his way back to the interstate.

9

Sam rolled into Denver at just before three AM, but he knew better than to go to his own home. Lemmons was fully aware that Sam was on the case, and if he realized that Sam's entire family had suddenly decided to leave town, he'd naturally figure it was to protect them from whoever was involved in that case. It seemed to Sam that it might be wise to find somewhere else to catch some sleep. He pulled the Corvette into the parking lot of a national chain hotel and walked into the office to get a room, specifically asking for one toward the back of the building. He paid cash rather than using his credit cards, didn't bother giving his correct license plate number on the registration form, and moved his car to the darkest part of the parking lot. Hopefully, that would mean that no one would be able to find out where he was staying.

And then he slept. Sam had no sooner hit the pillow

than his eyes closed and he drifted off into heavy sleep. He had managed to set an alarm on his phone for eight AM, and silently dared anyone to wake him before that time.

The nice thing, Sam thought, about being so tired was that he didn't seem to dream. Dreams didn't usually trouble him much anyway, but the sleep was so much more restful without it. When the alarm went off, he woke refreshed and ready to start formulating a plan for the rest of the day.

The first step was a shower, and as soon as he'd taken care of that, he made his way to the continental breakfast room. A place like this one always had waffles, and Sam considered waffles to be one of the four basic food groups. Two waffles and three cups of coffee later, he was ready to start letting his brain tackle the daunting task of finding a solution to a nearly impossible problem.

Item one: Detective Jerry Lemmons had participated in and perhaps even orchestrated the murders of three teenagers.

Item two: there were at least four other police officers involved in the murders and the resulting cover-up, including officers named Slocum, Forsyth and Driscoll.

Item three: Marty Fletcher had inadvertently caught the entire episode on video.

Item four: Marty had shared his fears and concerns

with Tracy, who wanted to help him negotiate a solution that would keep him from getting killed.

Item five: Tracy had hidden Marty away in a motel, then approached Jerry Lemmons without realizing he was involved in the murders.

Item six: Marty had recognized Jerry Lemmons from the video, and had promised to deliver the video in exchange for their safety.

Item seven: Lemmons had left with Tracy, and the hotel desk clerk had said she seemed frightened.

Item eight: Tracy had called Marty that day and told him to go and hide, and hadn't been seen or heard from since.

Taking all of these things together, Sam agreed with Marty's conclusion that Jerry Lemmons was responsible for Tracy's disappearance, and was probably holding her somewhere to keep her quiet and use her as leverage whenever he managed to locate Marty, a tool to help him get his hands on the video. If that was true, then it was very likely that Tracy had been questioned, and probably tortured to some degree to try to get Marty's location from her. At some point, it was likely that the questioning would have turned to what else she might be planning, and it wasn't likely she could manage not to give up the fact that she had hoped to get Sam involved.

Of course, she never called Sam, herself. There was a good chance her maternal instincts would prevent her from telling Detective Lemmons that she had told her daughter to contact Sam if anything happened to her. A mother can endure a lot when it comes to protecting her children, Sam knew.

But then Sam had called Lemmons and asked about Tracy. It would be difficult for the detective not to put two and two together. Someone, and Heather would be the most likely person, had contacted Sam about Tracy. Would that put the girl in danger?

It could, Sam realized, but he doubted it was likely at that moment. A teenage girl's suspicions might be enough to engage a private investigator, but they wouldn't interest any other cops. As long as Tracy was missing but presumed to be alive, there was no reason for Lemmons to take any action with regard to the girl. If her body were to be found later, however, there was always the possibility that the police might remember her daughter's insistence that Tracy had been abducted. Heather would be in a lot more danger then.

* * * * *

Marty Fletcher was a coffee drinker, but that usually meant a trip to see the local barista. In the cabin, however, there was neither a microwave nor a coffee maker, so he scrounged through the cabinets until he came up with a jar of instant coffee, then fumbled around putting water in a teakettle and setting it on the old gas stove. It took him a minute to figure out that the gas wasn't going to light itself, and by then he had to open a door to let some of the fumes out. Finally, he found the box of matches and managed not to singe his eyebrows getting it lit.

Once the kettle began to whistle, he made himself a cup of coffee and carried it out onto the cabin's front porch. He'd never really been much of a nature buff, but he admitted to himself there was something serene about sitting in the wilderness, listening to the sounds of the mountain and forest around him. The morning breeze blew through the trees, squirrels scampered in their branches and what looked like a whole herd of deer wandered past. A couple of them looked directly at him, but they showed no fear as they gracefully strolled away.

There were many animal noises in the air, as well. He heard chirps and chitters, the bellowing of an elk and what he was sure must be the howl of a wolf. He leaned back on the rustic bench and closed his eyes, just taking in the various sounds.

Another noise broke into his consciousness, and it took him a second to realize that it was the sound of tires on gravel. A vehicle was coming up the road toward the cabin, and Marty hoped it might be Sam returning to tell him that Tracy was safe and everything was over. He sat forward on the bench and stared through the trees, hoping to spot the beautiful red Corvette.

It wasn't Sam. The vehicle coming up the road was

a car, a big silver one that should never have been on such a road. It was moving slowly, the driver being careful as he tried to avoid ruts and the bigger rocks. The hairs on the back of Marty's neck suddenly stood up, and somehow he knew the car represented danger.

He was up and inside the cabin a second later, watching through the window as the car approached. He was fairly sure he hadn't been seen by the driver, and kept telling himself it was possible the car was simply lost or going even further up the old road.

He didn't truly believe that, of course. No one who knew that road would deliberately drive up it in such a low-slung automobile unless it was absolutely necessary, as it had been for Sam the night before. When the car came into clear view and turned into the driveway of the cabin, Marty spun and bolted out the back.

Fifty yards behind the cabin, he stopped and huddled behind a tree. He heard two car doors open and close, and knew instantly that the occupants were looking for him. He could vaguely hear one of them knocking on the front door, as a second man circled around the cabin and came into view. Marty knew the face; it was one he could never forget. Officer Driscoll was sneaking up toward the back door of the cabin, a revolver in one hand and a cell phone in the other.

"We found him," Driscoll said into the phone. "He's been hiding out in Prichard's cabin. Yeah, his van is out front, and the lights are on in the cabin..."

Slocum suddenly came through the back door of the cabin. He looked out toward the woods, and for a moment Marty thought he'd been spotted. "He's around here somewhere," Slocum said. "Cup of coffee on the table was still warm."

Driscoll looked around at the woods. "Looks like he took off into the forest," he said. "Don't worry, we'll find him. Yeah, I know, I said don't worry. We'll take care of him." He cut the call and put the phone in his pocket, then he and Slocum started walking toward the trees.

Doing his best to stay quiet, Marty turned and made his way through the trees, moving further up the mountain. He'd gone a dozen steps when he stepped on a dry, broken branch, and the loud crack that it made sounded almost like a gunshot in his ears.

"Marty?" Driscoll called out. "Marty, we know you're here. Come on out, we just want to talk to you."

Marty ran. Behind him, he could hear the two cops crashing through the forest in pursuit.

* * * * *

Sam decided it was time to put his plan into action, so he checked out of the hotel and got into his car. No one seemed to be paying any attention to him as he drove out of the parking lot, headed toward District One and the Major Crimes Unit. He took out his phone and dialed the number as he drove.

"Denver police, this is Sergeant Ragsdale, how may I help you?"

"Sergeant, this is Sam Prichard," Sam said. "I'd like to speak to Jerry Lemmons, please."

"Just one moment, sir," the sergeant said. Sam heard the hold music for a moment, and then Lemmons's voice came on the line.

"Detective Lemmons."

"Jerry, it's Sam Prichard. Remember that situation I called you about yesterday?"

Sam didn't detect any nervousness in the detective's voice. "Yeah, Tracy Jensen. Have you heard anything about her? We're still thinking she just ran off with her boyfriend."

"No you're not," Sam said. "I've got a hunch you know exactly where she is, and I've got what you're actually looking for. Think maybe we ought to get together and talk this over?"

Lemmons chuckled. "Not sure what you're thinking," he said, "but I'd be glad to get together over a cup of coffee, if you want. Name the time and place."

Sam spotted a Denny's restaurant just ahead. "How about Denny's on Federal? I'm pulling in now, I'll get us a table off by ourselves where we can talk."

"Sounds good," the detective said. "I'll be there in about fifteen minutes. Order me a cup of coffee, would you?" The line went dead, and Sam slipped his phone back into his pocket as he parked the car. He tucked the tablet into the back of his pants and let his polo shirt hang down over it.

Sam flashed his ID and told the hostess that he needed a table where he and a police detective could talk privately, so she showed him to a booth in a back room that was normally reserved for parties. There was no one else in the room, so the hostess took his order for two cups of coffee and brought them back just a moment later, then left him alone again.

Lemmons showed up in less than twelve minutes, told the hostess he was meeting someone, and was shown back to Sam's booth in the far corner of the back room. Sam didn't bother to rise as he approached and slid into the opposite side.

"I just love Denny's coffee, don't you?" he asked, smiling at Sam.

"It's okay," Sam said. He watched the hostess as she left the room, then turned his gaze directly onto Lemmons. "Let's cut to the chase, shall we? I've seen the video, and I know what you did. It doesn't take a genius to figure out you got Tracy stashed somewhere, so I'm here to negotiate for her release."

The smile never wavered. "What video you talking about? I'm afraid you've lost me, Sam."

"You, Driscoll, Slocum and Forsyth," Sam said, "plus another cop I didn't recognize. Three dead kids. Sound familiar now?"

Lemmons shrugged. "I've heard a rumor about something like this, but if such a video exists, I've yet to see it. I'm afraid that makes me wonder if you've actually seen it, or if you're just hearing the same rumors I've heard."

Sam shook his head. "Don't try to play me, Jerry. We both know exactly what I'm talking about, and we both know what will happen if I take it to the right people. Now, my client only wants her mother back, she doesn't give a royal flying you-know-what about you or anybody else. I've not only seen the video, I've got it, the only existing copy. You give me Tracy, I'll give it to you and this whole thing fades into history."

The detective leaned his elbows on the table and looked Sam in the eye. "Assuming for the sake of argument that what you're saying actually makes any sense, would you really expect me to believe that none of these people would talk about what they saw on this imaginary video? I mean, it might be hard to prove, but it still wouldn't be good for my career, now would it?"

"They'll stay quiet," Sam said. "While talking about it might be bad for your career, I think they understand it would be a lot worse for them and their loved ones, wouldn't you think? Let's face it, they know just what you're capable of."

Lemmons stared at Sam for a moment, then shrugged. "And what about you? Would you be content to just let it go?"

Sam grinned at him, but it was made of ice. "There was a time when Tracy was very important to me," he said. "I've moved on since then, but I still don't want any harm to come to her. You give me Tracy, unharmed, along with your word that none of us will ever be bothered about this again, and I give you the video. That's the deal, take it or leave it. If we leave this table without an agreement, then I'll do what I have to do. I think we understand each other."

Lemmons sat in silence for a moment, his own smile slowly fading from his face. "I think we do," he said. "The trouble is, Sam, I don't think you can hold up your end of the bargain. See, the thing about a video is that it's just too easy to make copies. Anybody in the position you seem to think you have me in would be stupid to give up whatever leverage he has, at least without being certain that no other copies were going to turn up in the future. Any idea how you could reassure someone about that?"

"There aren't any other copies," Sam said, "just one on a tablet. Marty said he was afraid to make copies, so he put it on the tablet and encrypted it so that it can't even be copied or emailed to anybody. It's the only one, and I have it put away safe. I'll hand it over in return for Tracy and your assurance that none of you will ever bother any of us again."

Lemmons's phone rang, and he held up a finger to tell Sam to wait a moment, then took out the phone and answered it. "Detective Lemmons," he said. "Yes? Well, that's excellent news. All right, thanks for letting me know." He ended the call and slipped his phone back into its case on his belt, then looked at Sam.

"Sam," he said, "that call was from one of the men in a special unit that I run. It seems you and I might have something to talk about after all."

Sam's eyebrows rose slightly. "Really? And what might that be?"

Lemmons smiled broadly. "Well, it seems that Marty Fletcher was just found. Unfortunately, he's dead, and since his body was found near a cabin that happens to belong to you, I'm afraid I'm going to have to place you under arrest for his murder."

10

Sam's blood went cold as his mind began racing. He cocked his head to one side and stared Lemmons in the eye. "You son-of-a-bitch," he said. "What did you do, follow us there and wait for me to leave?"

"Nah, nothing so dramatic. It turns out Marty bought that van from one of those 'buy here, pay here,' used-car dealers. They put GPS trackers into every vehicle they sell, so they can find it if you decide not to pay and take off with it. We got the code for his tracker last week, and we've been keeping an eye on him ever since. When he suddenly moved off to the middle of nowhere, I sent one of my officers out to check on him. Imagine his surprise when he found Marty lying on the floor of your hunting cabin, his head all smashed in. Is that how you got the video from him? Beat on him until he gave it up?" He waggled the barrel of his gun. "Now, very carefully, take out your pistol and pass it to me, butt first. You try anything else, I'll blow you away right here."

Sam silently cursed himself for choosing a booth, leaving him trapped in between the table and the wall behind him. He carefully removed his Glock from its holster and handed it over. "We both know I didn't kill him," he said, "though I'm sure you're going to do your best to make it look that way. Of course, if you take me in, then I'll have more than an ample opportunity to turn that video over to the right people. Sure you want to take that chance?"

Lemmons's smile was back and as bright as ever. "Well, let's see," he said. "You said you got the only remaining copy of the video, but you stashed it somewhere safe. Knowing you, I bet there's no one else in the world who knows where it is right now. That means the chances of it turning up are pretty slim, right? All I've got to do is make sure you don't get the chance to tell anyone where you hid it." He moved quickly, and suddenly had his service automatic in his hand. "Slide out of your seat, Sam, and stand up slowly. Keep your hands up where I can see them and turn your back to me."

Sam nodded. "Sure," he said, "so you can let everybody here see you arresting me? Then, let me guess, somewhere between here and the jail, I'm going to try to escape, right? You had no choice but to shoot me, right?"

The detective nodded back. "You see, I knew you were smart. In fact, you're smart enough to figure out that if you don't cooperate with me now, there's a good possibility that some of the innocent parties between us and the door might be hurt, too. I'm pretty sure you won't want that to happen, so let's just play this out by my rules. You get up, let me cuff you and take your gun, and then we go out to my car. But instead of me shooting you when you try to escape, how about you just take me right to that video? Once I've got that, you're no longer a threat to me or anyone else."

"And what about the murder charge? Does that go away?"

Lemmons shrugged at him. "I could probably see my way clear to saying I checked out your alibi and it was good. Sam, all I want is that video. You hand it over now, and I can let you walk. As long as you and I never cross paths on this again, you got nothing to worry about."

Sam sighed and began sliding toward the end of the seat. "And what about Tracy? Let me have her in the deal, and I'll go for it. That's all I really wanted anyway."

"Do you really think you can keep her mouth shut? That's all that matters to me, and you know it."

Sam stood, his hands held out to his sides and slightly raised. "Of course I can. She's got a kid, she'd know how easily you could hurt her daughter if she ever talked. Believe me, she won't say a word."

Lemmons motioned with the gun for Sam to turn around. "Fine," he said. "I'll tell you what. I'm going to put my gun away, and you and I are going to walk out of here like two old friends. Hell, I'll even pay for the coffee, how about that? When we get outside, you just climb into the car with me and we'll go get the video, then we'll go pick up Tracy. I'll drop the two of you off back here at your car, and that'll be the end of it. That work for you?"

Sam turned his head and looked back over his shoulder. "Sure," he said. "At this point, you've got all the cards. We'll do it your way."

"Okay, but just remember," Lemmons said. "You make one wrong move, you try anything, and some of these innocent folks are going to get hurt. Play it cool and everything will be over pretty quick."

Lemmons slipped his gun back into the holster under his jacket, and he and Sam started toward the front of the restaurant. When they stepped through into the main dining room, they almost ran into the hostess who was on her way back to them with a fresh pot of coffee.

"Oh, excuse me," she said. "I thought you guys might be ready for a refill."

"No, thanks," Lemmons said. "We got some things to go take care of, but we appreciate you letting us have the space back there." They followed her back to the register, and Lemmons took out his wallet. "How much we owe you, sweetie?"

The girl picked up a ticket. "That'll be three fifty-seven, altogether."

Lemmons reached into his wallet and took out a ten-dollar bill, handed it to the girl and told her to keep the change. She smiled and thanked him, and then he followed Sam out the front door. "That's my car," he said, pointing at an unmarked Dodge. Sam started toward it, then leaned hard on his cane as his hip appeared to falter on him.

Lemmons stopped and looked at him, but Sam motioned that he was okay. Lemmons stepped past him, and that's when Sam yanked the cane up off the ground and grasped it by the lower shaft. He swung it like a baseball bat, and the heavy metal handle caught Lemmons on his left ear.

Lemmons let out a squeal of pain, and fell to the ground. Sam's pistol fell out of where he'd tucked it into his belt, and Sam snatched it up and aimed it at the detective's head.

"We could have done this the easy way, Jerry, but you had to be the tough guy. Very carefully, I want you to take your pistol out and lay it on the ground. You even look like you're going to try anything, I'll blow your head off."

"Shit," Lemmons yelled. "You really think you can get away with shooting a cop in cold blood? People are staring through the windows, you idiot, they see you pointing a gun at an unarmed man. You shoot me, you go down for murdering a cop."

"Not likely," Sam said. "Remember that video? I'm pretty sure that's all I need to convince a jury I was acting in good faith and self-defense. Now, put your gun on the ground, and I mean right now."

Lemmons glared at him, but then he carefully inserted two fingers into his jacket and pulled the pistol out. He gave it a slight toss and it clattered on the ground near Sam's feet.

Sam reached down and picked it up, shoving it into the waistband of his pants. "All right, now, get up slowly and put your hands on the hood of the car."

Lemmons took his hand off his car and glanced at it, scowling when he saw blood. "Geez, you split my freaking ear."

"Shut up and spread 'em," Sam said. "Hands on the hood, like I told you. Come on, you know the drill."

Lemmons got slowly to his feet and put his hands on the car, scooting his feet backward and spreading them wide. Sam used one of his own to kick them a little further apart, then began patting the detective down, looking for other weapons he might have hidden on his body. All he found was a pocketknife and the keys to the Dodge.

He took the handcuffs that were in a case on the back of the detective's belt. "Left hand, put it behind your back," he said.

Lemmons suddenly thrust himself backward and Sam instinctively raised the barrel of the gun toward the sky, taking it off the detective's head. Lemmons spun and grabbed at it; he missed, but he had thrown Sam off balance, and the bad hip screamed at being twisted in a direction it wasn't meant to go. Sam fell back into a bush in front of the restaurant, and Lemmons took off running. By the time Sam got back on his feet, the man had raced around the end of the building. Sam hurried over the best he could, but Lemmons was completely out of sight.

Within seconds, Sam knew, Lemmons would be on the phone and doing everything he could to turn Sam Prichard into a target. It wasn't even just the dirty cops Sam needed to worry about. Once the notion that Sam had killed Marty and then attacked a police detective started spreading around the department, just about any cop would consider him dangerous enough to want to shoot first and ask the questions later.

Sam hurried to the Corvette, but he glanced at the windows of the restaurant to see a dozen people staring at him. There would be squad cars on the way there any second, and the stories these witnesses would tell would not look good. His carefully laid-out plan in shambles, Sam decided the best thing he could do was simply get out of sight.

He got into the car and backed out of his parking

space, then drove quickly out onto Federal Boulevard. Common sense told him to get off the main streets as quickly as possible, so he took a quick right onto Sixteenth Street and followed it a couple of miles, until he got to Meade. Another right turn took him up to Eighteenth, where he turned left toward West Lakeshore Drive. Lakeshore was more of a park road that simply followed the eastern edge of Sloan's Lake, and didn't get a lot of traffic. He pulled to the side of the street and parked beside a stand of trees.

After some of Sam's previous cases had gotten a lot of press, there were probably very few cops in the entire Metro area who didn't know who he was, or would fail to spot his flashy, candy-apple-red Corvette. There weren't many 'Vettes like his in the area, anyway, but the custom paint job he had painstakingly applied made it almost a one-of-a-kind. There was no doubt the first squad car that spotted it would turn and give chase.

First things first, then, he thought, *time to ditch the car.* He knew it would be impounded as soon as it was found, which meant it would be safe for a while, so he climbed out and started walking away from the lake. Keeping his eyes peeled for any sign of police, he made his way back to Eighteenth and turned left. There was an RTD bus stop just a couple of blocks in that direction, and public transportation sounded like the best way to put distance between him and the car.

He made it to the bus stop with only minutes to spare, and climbed on as soon as it arrived. Sam still kept a valid bus pass, a habit he'd gotten into after his forced retirement. His motorcycle had broken down on him twice, leaving him stranded miles from home; the second time, he decided keeping a bus pass in his wallet would be a smart move.

He made his way down the aisle and plopped into a seat toward the rear of the bus. There was, of course, the risk he might be recognized; between the high-profile cases he'd solved that got his picture in the newspaper and his current moderate fame as a singer, there were plenty of people in the city who might know him on-sight, but buses are like elevators. Most people try not to notice who else is riding with them, and he was counting on that little tidbit of human nature to help him out at the moment.

Apparently, he still had some luck on his side. There were only a handful of people on the bus and all of them were busy reading or looking out the window. Sitting where he was toward the rear, there was a greatly reduced chance of anyone noticing him.

He took out his phone and started scanning local news stories. None of them seemed to pertain to him, or to Marty, so he assumed no announcement had yet been made concerning his being a murder suspect. Considering what he knew about normal police procedure, he figured the first public announcement would come with the noon news updates. That meant he had at least a couple of hours before everything hit the fan.

Sam leaned back in the seat and tried to think. If Lemmons was telling the truth, and Marty was dead, then it was likely the video on the Internet would never be seen again. That meant the copy on the tablet really was the only one, now. No matter what else happened, Sam had to see to it that it got to someone who would take the appropriate action against Lemmons and his dirty cops.

Sam Prichard trusted very few people in this world, and something this big made that list even smaller. He toyed with the idea of calling his old friend Harry Winslow, but Harry was a big shot with Homeland Security in DC, nowadays. Sam was certain he'd do whatever it took to help, but some residual loyalty to the Denver PD, where Sam had spent ten years of his life, made him want to keep this matter local. That left him with only one possibility: Karen Parks.

11

Karen was a homicide detective, but she had once been Sam's partner in the juvenile division. Since his retirement and entry into the world of private investigations, they had worked together on several cases and Sam felt he could trust her completely.

He glanced down at his hand and realized he was still holding his phone, so he scrolled through his contacts and punched her name with his thumb. It rang twice before she answered.

"Detective Parks," she said. "I saw the caller ID, so I know who this is. You want to tell me what in the Sam Hill is going on?"

She realized who was calling, but was carefully not using his name. That told him that Lemmons was already spreading the word that Sam was wanted for murder. He whispered a prayer of thanks that Karen knew him well enough to want to hear his side of the story before she accepted it as truth.

"You bet I do," Sam said, "but you're not gonna believe it. I just need to know something. Do you honestly believe I could do what I'm accused of?"

Sam heard her sigh. "If it was anybody but you on this phone, I'd lie and say what they wanted to hear. Since it's you, though, I can be honest. Hell, no, I don't believe it."

"Thanks. You are about the only person in this whole city I trust at the moment, so that means a lot to me."

"Glad I can help you feel better," Karen said. "Now, what is this all about?"

"Right at this moment, telling you would only put you in danger. I know you, Karen, you'd want to do something about it the same way I do, but you have to believe me when I tell you this is too big to handle on our own. I'm not sure what to do with it just yet, but I needed to know that there was someone inside the department I can trust."

"Well, you can trust me. Can you give me some idea of how I can help?"

"Not just yet. I'm probably going to need information pretty soon, though, things you may need to find out for me. For right at the moment, just don't let anyone know you've spoken to me, okay? The people behind my current situation wouldn't hesitate to try to use you or your kids against me, or they might just decide they want you out of the way."

She was silent for a moment. "Okay, we'll play this your way. I'll keep all of this between us. But, Sam, if you're worried about me and my family, what about your own?"

"I've already got them out of town, and even I don't know where they are. You know Indie, nobody's going to track her down unless she wants them to. They're safe for the moment." He thought for a few seconds. "What have you heard about what's going on?"

"Jerry Lemmons says you were digging around in his missing persons investigation and somehow got crossways with some guy named Fletcher. Story is, you took Fletcher out to some old cabin you own and killed him, then hid his body in the woods. He's claiming he's got enough for a murder charge, but the DA hasn't agreed to it yet."

"Okay, that's a relief for the moment, anyway. I'm gonna need to ditch this phone shortly, but I'll round up another one as quick as I can and call you. Let me know if they decide to make it official, okay?"

"You'll know as soon as I do, or at least as soon as I talk to you again. Just tell me why Jerry is out to get you, can you do that?"

"Again, the less you know, the better off you are. Let's leave it at that for now, and I'll tell you as soon as I possibly can." He looked up and saw that they were approaching a stop at a shopping center. "Gotta go for now," he said. "I'll have a new phone pretty quick, call you then."

He ended the call and stood as the bus came to a stop, turning off his phone and shoving it under the seat, jamming it into the framework. With any luck, no one would notice it for quite some time. He stepped off the bus and mingled with the milling crowd that was heading into the mall.

It took him only fifteen minutes to find Gadgets, a store that specialized in electronics. A young man with spiky hair smiled at him as he entered.

"Welcome to Gadgets," he said. "My name is Joel. What can I do for you today?"

Sam gave him a grin and spoke in an accent that sounded like it came from somewhere in the Appalachians. "Hi, there, I'm Wendell. I'm here visiting my sister and my dad gum cell phone broke, can you believe that? I can't get a new one until I get home, so I thought I'd come see about one of those cheap ones. Y'all sell those?"

Joel squinted one eye. "Uh, yeah. You want something simple, or a smart phone with a data plan?"

"Oh, nothing fancy. With my luck, the phone would be smarter than me. How about one of those easy ones that just make phone calls?"

Sam chose the simplest phone the store kept in stock, and it took another fifteen minutes to get it activated. Within forty minutes of entering the mall, he was making his first call as he walked out a rear entrance.

"Hello?" Indie said.

"It's me, Babe. Just thought it was time to check in."

"Sam? I didn't know the number, what happened to your phone?"

"I decided to get rid of mine for now, too," he said. "I'll be using this one for the time being. You guys doing okay?"

"Me? I'm lounging beside a pool while our mothers are splashing in the water with our daughter. How are things on your end?"

"Same old things," Sam said. "I confronted a killer this morning, and now I'm wanted for murder. Typical day."

Sam could hear her eyebrows trying to crawl over the top of her scalp. "Wanted for *murder*? Sam, what on earth have you gotten into?"

"Well, I had stashed Marty Fletcher out at Dad's old hunting cabin, I thought he'd be safe there. Unfortunately, Lemmons and his boys tracked him down by some GPS thing in his van. Lemmons is claiming he's dead, and the word is out that I supposedly killed him. Probably be a good idea for you to stay wherever you are for a few more days, at least."

"Oh, my God, Sam, did Lemmons kill him?"

"Not personally, but he's definitely involved and it gets even worse than that. I'm not going into detail over the phone, but there is no doubt in my mind he'll kill me if he gets a chance."

Indie was quiet for a few seconds, then spoke. "What about Tracy? Have you found anything on her?"

"Not yet, but I think she's still alive. Marty Fletcher had something Lemmons wanted, and I'm pretty sure he was using Tracy as leverage to get it. Now he knows that I've got it, and that he'll never get it if anything happens to her. I'm hoping that will be enough to keep her alive until I can get to the bottom of this."

"And just how on earth are you planning to do that, without getting yourself killed in the process?"

"Right now, I'm going to make myself the biggest possible thorn in Jerry Lemmons's side. I've got somebody who's willing to work with me on it, somebody I trust. The idea is to keep Lemmons and his accomplices hopping until I find out where Tracy is. I'll give you a call in a few hours, let you know what's going on, okay?"

Indie sighed. "Sam, this is scary. Beauregard said there were three lives to save, and if Marty is already dead..."

"I know. If that's one down, who are the other two? I don't suppose Beauregard has had anything more to say about it?" Sam heard the catch in Indie's voice, as if she started to say something and then thought better of it. "What? Tell me."

She let out an even deeper sigh. "I'm not sure it means anything," she said, "which is why I hadn't mentioned it. Mom says Beauregard told her a little while ago that you're going to have to figure out how to solve this case all on your own."

"All on my own? What on earth is that supposed to mean?"

"Honey, like I said, I don't know that it means anything. I mean, of course you got to solve it on your own, there's nobody else who can do it, right?"

It was Sam's turn to sigh. "None of this is making any sense at all," he said. "I'll call you when I can. Love you, Babe."

"I love you too," Indie said. "You be careful, okay?" The phone went dead.

His next call was to Karen Parks. "It's me," he said. "Keep this number. Any news?"

"Not just yet," she replied. "I can tell you that every cop out there is keeping an eye out for you, but I bet you already knew that."

"Standard procedure. Okay, just let me know if anything new develops."

"Not so fast, there, Buster. Your car was located a few minutes ago, and is being towed in. How are you going to get around while you're trying to clear your name?"

"Guess I'll keep riding the bus. No other options, at the moment."

"Well, I've got one for you. My dad's old pickup truck is sitting behind my house. If you trust me, tell me where you are and I'll come get you. You can use the truck for a while."

"I trust you," Sam said, "but are you sure you want to take the chance? If this goes sour, it won't look good that you let me use a vehicle."

"So don't let it go sour. Tell me where to meet you, and I'll get there as quick as I can."

Sam sighed and told her to meet him in the parking lot of one of the big department stores at the mall. She said she'd be there in twenty minutes, and hung up the phone.

Sam leaned nervously against a dumpster beside the building until he spotted Karen's unmarked Charger cruising slowly through the parking lot. He stepped out where she could see him and waited for her to pull alongside, then jumped into the passenger seat.

"Hunker down, would you?" Karen asked. "Last thing I need is for anyone to spot you in here with me at the moment. Damn, Sam, you get yourself into some of the worst messes. We've got a few minutes, why don't you start telling me what the hell is going on?"

Sam slunk down low in the seat and grinned up at her. "Remember I said you weren't going to like it? Well, here's the short version. Long time ago, I was engaged to a girl who had been my best friend all the way through school. Things fell apart, for reasons we don't need to worry about anymore, and the engagement got called off. Well, she disappeared a few days ago and yesterday, her teenage daughter came to see me. The girl says her mom told her that if anything were to happen to her, she was supposed to come and get me to look into it."

"Missing woman? You're talking about that Tracy Jensen? Jerry Lemmons has that case, and he's the one claiming you murdered some guy named Fletcher. I'm guessing this is all connected, then?"

"Like a big jigsaw puzzle," Sam said. "Marty Fletcher was a video blogger, one of those guys who talks to a camera and then posts it up on YouTube. Apparently, the more followers you get, the more money you can make doing that kind of stuff. Fletcher had a lot of followers, but a couple of weeks ago he made a video and then forgot to turn off his camera. He left his van in a parking lot facing an alley, and a few hours later that camera captured five cops murdering three teenagers."

Karen's face spun around to look at him, her eyes wide. "You can't be serious!"

Sam nodded. "I'm dead serious, I've seen the video. There were four uniform cops, including Dave Forsyth who used to be in vice. Two of the others were named Slocum and Driscoll, but I never got a name on the fourth. The last one was none other than Detective Jerry Lemmons."

Karen kept her eyes on the road, but the set of her jaw told Sam she was having a hard time accepting what he was telling her. "You got some idea why they killed these kids?"

"I think it was just something that got out of control," Sam said. "Lemmons and some of the others were smacking two boys around, supposedly trying to teach them respect for law enforcement. Another cop was holding a girl that was with the boys, but she started screaming. Lemmons told that cop to shut her up, and I think he just meant to put her to sleep but he didn't let go quick enough. They suddenly realized she was dead, and then Lemmons said they had to finish the boys off and get rid of the bodies. They strangled the boys as well, then wrapped them up in a tarp and loaded them into the trunk of one of the squads."

Karen made a turn, then glanced at Sam again. "You think they killed Fletcher and the woman?"

"I'm sure they must've killed Fletcher. I tracked him down yesterday, and that's when he showed me the video. He was scared to death Lemmons and the others were going to kill him, so I took him to my dad's old cabin to hide him out. I was hoping to keep him safe, but they found him there and killed him, and Jerry wants to pin it on me. I'm still holding out hope that Tracy is alive."

"Let me guess," Karen said, "you told Lemmons you saw the video, right?"

"Yep, but it gets even better. I also told him that I've got the only copy. My plan was to try to convince him to give up Tracy in exchange for it, but Fletcher had another copy stashed on the Internet somewhere, don't know where. If he's dead, the one I've got really is the only one that's accessible. After I escaped from Lemmons at the restaurant, I'm sure he's telling everyone how dangerous I am, and that they need to shoot first and ask questions later. He's hoping I hid that video so well no one can find it, so if he can get rid of me, the problem goes away."

"And did you hide it?"

Sam pulled the tablet out from under the back of his shirt. "Not exactly," he said. "To be honest, I'm afraid to let it out of my possession."

12

Sam could see Karen's mind working hard, trying to make sense of everything she'd been told. Karen Parks was a good cop, and Sam knew that she'd have a hard time dealing with the idea of cold-blooded killers wearing badges.

She suddenly slowed the car down and turned carefully into an alley. A moment later, she pulled into her own backyard and parked next to an old Ford pickup truck.

"We're good here," she said. "Nobody can see inside my yard. Bring that damn tablet and follow me."

She climbed out of the car and Sam followed her into her house. She called out to be sure neither of her kids was home, then motioned for Sam to follow her into the living room. They sat down on the couch and she looked at Sam. "Show me."

Sam turned on the tablet and poked the icon. A

chime went off, and then the image of the alleyway appeared on the screen with a Play Button superimposed over it. Sam touched it to start the video running, then turned it so Karen could also see what was on the screen.

The video played through just as it had before, and Sam realized that he was noticing little details that had escaped him the first time. He hadn't noticed, for instance, that the girl was wearing clothes that suggested her family was well off, while the boys were dressed in what his mother would have referred to as "Salvation Army rejects." He couldn't help wondering how the three of them had ended up in that alley that night, but those were answers he could look for at a later time.

Sam pointed out Forsyth when he arrived, but told Karen he didn't know his partner's name. She leaned forward as the man came into view and said, "That's Mark Wright. He asked me for a date last week, but I turned him down. It's funny, he and Forsyth just got transferred to the day shift about ten days ago. In fact, so did these other two." She felt a shiver run down her spine. "Sure glad I didn't go out with him."

Sam kept watching and noticed something else. At the point where Jerry Lemmons arrived on the scene, Officer Driscoll's face broke into a smile, and the man actually winked. He was holding the girl's right arm in his right hand, but his left arm was already curling around her throat at that point. It almost looked like that he knew what was coming and was excited about it.

Karen sat perfectly still as the video played through, and when it finished she simply stared at the screen for another full minute. When she finally turned her face toward Sam, he could see the tears that were brimming over and beginning to run down her cheeks.

"Dear God, Sam," she said. "Dear God, they were just kids!"

Sam nodded. "Yeah, they were. I remember a couple of weeks ago, there was mention of a missing girl on the news. Her parents seemed to think she had run away with a couple of boys she was hanging out with. I suspect we've just seen the truth of what happened to her. As for the boys, I gather no one thinks much about them going missing."

Karen shook her head. "I vaguely remember something about the girl disappearing with two teenage boys, but that's all. From the look of those two, though, they might be the type that don't get noticed a lot. Boys like that can vanish without anyone raising too big a fuss."

"The problem is that this really is the only usable copy of the video, now. I need it to get Tracy back, but somehow we also have to get it to a prosecutor. Trouble is, the way he encrypted it, I can't even make a copy."

Karen grinned. "Someday when your daughter is a teenager, you'll learn a few tricks like the one I'm about to show you. Start that video again." She took out her phone, turned on its video camera app and pointed it at the screen of the tablet. When the video finished running, she saved the recording she had just made and then played part of it back. "It's a little grainy, but I bet we can find a computer guy who can clean it up pretty good, enough to show the grand jury."

Sam shook his head. "I'm married to a computer whiz, but I never would've thought of that. What are you going to do with it?"

"Monica Purvis is still bucking to run for governor one of these days," Karen said. "She'd be all over this. I'll get it to her and get her started on it. What are you going to be doing in the meantime?"

Sam thought for a moment. "Do me a favor and hold off on going to Purvis for a few hours. As far as Lemmons knows, I have the only existing copy. That's still the best hope I have of getting Tracy back alive to her family."

Karen looked up at him and smiled, but it didn't reach her eyes. "It's almost eleven, now. I'll give you until four o'clock, okay? That way I can catch her before she gets out of her office."

Sam nodded again. "Okay. Hopefully, that will be enough time. Just make sure nobody finds out you've got that video until after you talk to her. Lemmons won't hesitate to kill anyone he thinks is standing in the way of putting this behind him."

"Yeah," Karen said. "And at the moment, he figures that's just you." She reached into her purse and pulled out a set of keys, then grabbed a baseball cap that was lying on the coffee table. "Put this on and take the truck," she said. "It's not the most beautiful thing you'll ever drive, but it runs great and has plenty of power. Got a plan in mind yet?"

Sam put on the hat, added his own sunglasses and gave her his most evil grin. "The only one that ever really seems to work," he said. "I'm just going to use myself as bait."

Karen stared at him for a moment, then shook her head. "You know your wife is going to kill you if you live through this, right?"

Sam chuckled. "Let's just hope she gets the chance," he said as he walked out the back door and headed toward the old Ford. He glanced around to be sure no one was looking, then slid in behind the wheel. Lemmons's gun, still tucked into his waistband in the back, was pressing on his spine. He took it out and put it in the glove box.

Sam slid the key into the ignition and started the truck, backing out into the alley and following it for a couple of blocks before turning onto a side street. He made his way along between rows of houses with manicured lawns for about twenty minutes, putting distance between himself and Karen's house, then punched in the code to block caller ID and dialed the number for the Denver Police Department.

"I need to speak to Detective Lemmons," Sam said with a growl. "Tell him it's Sam Prichard."

The desk sergeant almost seemed to choke for a second, but then Sam heard the hold music. It took a couple of moments, but finally the call was transferred to Lemmons's cell phone.

"What do you want, Sam?"

"Same thing I wanted before," Sam said. "I've still got what you want, safely stashed away. I'll make the same trade we talked about earlier."

Lemmons was quiet for a moment. "We can negotiate. Since I'm sure you don't want this conversation recorded, give me your direct number and I'll call you."

"Very funny," Sam said. "You give me yours. I'm not going to let you have time to track my GPS signal."

Grudgingly, Lemmons told Sam his number and ended the call. Sam waited a few seconds and then punched it into his throwaway phone.

"So how do you want to do this?" Lemmons asked. "Face-to-face? There's an old empty apartment building at Wadsworth and Florida. That's where you'll find me in fifteen minutes."

Sam thought for a moment. "Okay," he said. "Come alone. Otherwise, I vanish and the video goes to the DA."

"Fifteen minutes," Lemmons said. "I'll be there, and I'll be alone. No guns, right, Sam?"

"That part's entirely up to you." Sam ended the call and took the next left. The intersection Lemmons had mentioned was to the south, and Sam was less than fifteen minutes from it. He pushed the old truck and made it there in ten.

The old four-story building was surrounded by a chain link fence, and signs announced that traffic would be rerouted two blocks around it the following day because it was scheduled to be demolished in order to make way for a new medical clinic. Lemmons wasn't there yet, so Sam parked the truck behind a large excavator on a trailer and shoved the tablet up under the seat of the truck, then got out and stood where he could look around the trailer and watch for Lemmons.

He took out his cell phone and dialed Indie, to let her know where he was and that he was meeting to talk with Lemmons, but nothing happened. He held the phone up and waved it around, but it was getting no service for some reason. He put it back into his pocket, frustrated, and continued to watch for Lemmons.

The detective arrived a few minutes later, and Sam peeked around the excavator long enough to be sure the man was alone and that no other cars were following. He waited a full minute, then stepped put and walked directly toward Lemmons's car.

Lemmons opened his door and got out, then closed

the door and leaned on it as he faced Sam. "Well," he said, "here we are again."

"Yeah," Sam said. "Where we could've been several hours ago, if you weren't such an idiot. I told you, Jerry, all I want is Tracy. She's not going to talk, simply because I can convince her it's the only way to keep her daughter safe. This whole thing can end without any more bloodshed."

Lemmons stared at him for a moment, then slowly shook his head. "I wish I could believe you, Sam," he said, "but there's just too much at stake. I can't risk everything on the notion that none of you will ever talk about this."

"Then give me another option," Sam said. "Give me something that'll let me bring Tracy home to her kid. Any idea what that might be?"

The detective stood there in silence for another few seconds, then nodded. "First off, you need to understand that this isn't quite what you think it is. Nobody wanted those kids to get killed, that wasn't the idea. It was supposed to go down different, with nobody really getting hurt at all. Driscoll just got carried away, and then it was too late."

Sam was surprised, but then he suddenly remembered the look on Driscoll's face when Lemmons had appeared, and how he'd thought it odd the officer already had his arm wrapped around the girl's throat at that time. From what Lemmons was saying, it almost sounded like the kids had been set up, somehow.

"It was planned," Sam said. "How? What was the whole point of it? Some way or another, you knew those kids were going to be there. What was supposed to happen, Jerry?"

Lemmons hesitated for another moment, but then went on. "The girl. She's been running with them boys lately, getting herself into trouble. They were smoking dope, stealing stuff, the usual kinds of trouble kids get themselves into, you know? Well, a couple days before that went down, I get a phone call. Her grandpa is a very powerful man in the city, and he wanted her to get scared straight, right? He went to somebody who calls me and tells me if I can pull that off, it'll be made well worth my while, and we're talking not just money, but some pretty good career incentives, you might say. I said I'd see what I could do, then I talked to a couple guys and we started keeping an eye on them. When we found a way to get them off by themselves, we were planning to rough the boys up and scare the girl real good, make sure she wouldn't risk letting any of us catch her out on the streets again. That was all it was supposed to be, I swear."

"But Driscoll got a little overzealous," Sam said. "Let me guess, he was supposed to put her in a sleeper hold, put her to sleep, right? By the time she woke up, those boys would be pretty bloodied, and you figured she'd run home to Mommy and Daddy and stay off the streets?"

Lemmons let out a sigh. "That was the idea," he said. "Then it just all fell apart. There was nothing I could do but try to clean up the mess."

"Oh, bull, Jerry," Sam said. "You could've called nine one one and told the truth. Paramedics might've been able to revive the girl, maybe it wasn't too late."

"You try to think at a moment like that!" Lemmons shouted suddenly. "I made the call that came to me at that moment, and if you want to know whether I regret it or not, hell, yes, I do. Every minute since then, I've tried to think of what else I could have done. If I'd just looked up at Driscoll a minute sooner, it all might have been different. You know how many times I wished I'd never agreed to get involved in this at all?"

"Okay, but now it's too late to undo it. Now we've got a total of four dead bodies. There's no point in anyone else having to die over this, Jerry. Tell me where Tracy is, let me at least bring her home to her daughter. I'll keep her quiet, I promise you."

"Stop saying that!" Lemmons yelled. "There's no way in the world you can guarantee she won't talk sooner or later, so if I give her up to you, I'm out of leverage. You want her, fine, let's talk about that. If I give her up, what will you give me in exchange? What do I get, a head start, maybe? A chance to run?"

"Would that be enough? Would that get me Tracy,

alive?" Sam asked.

There was a moment of silence, and then Lemmons spoke again, waving a hand for emphasis. "What if— what if there was another way? What if we could clean this whole thing up without that video ever seeing the light of day?"

Sam's eyes narrowed as he stared at the detective. "I'm listening," he said.

"You want Tracy Jensen back alive? Well, here's my offer. Without that video, there is no way to actually prove who did or said what that night. The tragedy of it all is that those kids are dead, right? Somebody needs to pay for that, right? How about this? I'll give you Driscoll and his partner. The rest of us will swear the kids were dead when we got there, and that Driscoll said they'd claim we were all in on it if we didn't help them cover it up. We panicked and screwed up, but that's all it was, just a big mistake. Driscoll and Slocum go down for the murders, the rest of us lose our jobs, maybe get some probation or something, and you get another big feather in your cap for cracking the case. How about it, Sam? I screwed up, I know it, but I don't want to throw my whole life away over it. I've got a wife, I've got two kids. I don't want to lose everything!"

Sam's gut was rumbling as he listened to Lemmons trying to twist the story into something that would keep him from facing the penalty he deserved. Still, it was a chance to get Tracy out alive. Sam tried to make it look like he was seriously considering the offer.

"All three of you would have to be able to tell the same story," Sam said. "How long would it take you to arrange that?"

Lemmons's voice suddenly had hope in it. "I can fix that up in a matter of minutes," he said. "Let me make a couple of calls, explain to them that this is the only way we get through this, and the three of us will meet you somewhere. I'll tell you where to find the woman, and you can take us in. It'll be your bust, and I can even set up Driscoll and Slocum so you can arrest them, too. All you gotta do is keep that video from ever turning up, and then if the Jensen woman ever decides to talk, it'll be her word against ours. Without any serious evidence to back it up, it won't even matter that Driscoll and Slocum would say she was telling the truth. What do you say, Sam?"

13

The window behind Lemmons suddenly exploded, and the detective's face took on a look of surprise. A bright red spot appeared on the front of his shirt and began spreading, running downward from the center of his chest. Sam stared in shock as Lemmons looked down at himself, then slowly sank to the ground.

The shot had come from a side street, and Sam spun and bolted around the building. A quick glance around the corner at Lemmons told him the man was dead, so Sam pulled his own pistol and leaned back against the old brick wall. His mind was racing, trying to figure out just what had happened.

Either Lemmons hadn't really come alone, or someone had followed him. Sam figured it was the latter, that at least one of the other cops—probably either Driscoll or Slocum—had somehow tailed him to the meeting and heard him trying to give them up.

Of course, that meant they also heard that Sam had the video. His own life was now on the line, he knew, and it wouldn't be long before the shooter came looking for him. He glanced around the corner again but saw no one, then hurried along the side of the building to the back and ducked low as he peeked out once more. There was still no one in sight, so Sam stood again and pressed his back to the bricks.

Straight in front of him was more of the chain link fence. It was at least six feet high, but there was a barrel standing beside it. Ignoring the pain in his hip, Sam hurried over and leapt up onto the barrel, then threw himself over the top of the fence. He landed hard in somebody's backyard and went down, but scrambled to his feet and began a limping run across it.

There was a wooden fence on the other side of the yard, but it was broken and Sam managed to climb through a hole. The yard he entered then was unfenced, but a large Rottweiler began barking at him and straining at the heavy chain that secured it to a doghouse. It couldn't reach him, so he kept moving from one backyard to the next until he came to the street at the end of the block.

He grabbed at his phone and looked at it, but it was still showing no bars. He tried calling Karen Parks anyway, but when it only beeped in failure, he shoved it back into his pocket once again.

From back toward the apartment building, he heard

an engine and squealing tires, so he turned to the left and found an alley leading back the way he'd come. He made it back to the chain link around the building, found an open gate and rushed inside, then hurried to where he'd left the pickup.

It had worked; the shooter hadn't expected him to double back. He made it to the truck and jumped inside, started it up and whispered a prayer of thanks for the big 460 that roared to life under the hood. He yanked the shifter into drive and floored it, racing out the exit from the apartment parking lot and onto South Wadsworth. He turned right at the first intersection, praying that he was moving away from the direction the shooter had been driving.

Five minutes later he saw no sign of pursuit, so he made a couple of turns and slowed to normal driving speeds. He took the phone out of his pocket, saw that it had service again and called Karen Parks.

"How's it going?" Karen asked nonchalantly as she answered.

"Lemmons is dead," Sam said. "We met at an old apartment building in Lakewood, and somebody shot him while we were talking. He told me that someone had contacted him a few weeks back and wanted him to scare that girl so she'd stop running the streets, and that he'd be rewarded if he succeeded. The others were supposed to help him with that but it all went wrong. He was trying to make a deal with me to hang Driscoll and Slocum for the murders and let the rest of them off as accessories after, and I suspect the shooter was one of them."

"Accessories? How did he figure to get away with that?"

"He wanted to tell a story that Driscoll and Slocum killed the kids, then threatened to involve the rest of them if they didn't help cover it up and they panicked and went along with it. Without the video, it would be their word against him and the other two, who would back him up."

"Oh, Geez! Where are you now?"

"Just driving around," he said. "The shooter was looking for me but I've shaken him, I think. I'm trying to think of what to do now, some other way to find Tracy."

"Okay, but try to stay out of sight. Lemmons was the one accusing you of murder, so if anyone saw the two of you together, you're going to be the number one suspect in his killing. Wait a minute, hang on..."

Her voice stopped and Sam could hear radio chatter in the background, but then she came back on the line. "Sam," she said, "I think maybe you're right about the shooters. Officers Driscoll and Slocum are currently securing the scene where Lemmons was shot. They claim he told them to follow him and watch from a distance while he tried to take you into custody, and that they saw you shoot him in cold blood. They say they fired shots at you, but you got away."

Sam shook his head, the impact of her words hitting him like a punch in the gut. "Karen, I swear I'm telling you the truth," he said. "I never..."

"Knock it off, Sam," she said. "I saw that video, remember? I know damn well you didn't kill Lemmons. Apparently they followed him on their own and overheard him talking to you. Of course they wanted him dead; if he was trying to set them up for the fall, that would be all the motive they could possibly need. Listen, I'm gonna call Monica and try to get this to her now, we can't wait any longer. I show her this video, she's going to get arrest warrants for all of these bastards within minutes, and we can question them then. One of them will undoubtedly know where your old girlfriend is being held. You just stay out of sight until I call you, got that?"

"I'll do my best," Sam said. "Or would it be better if I came with you, let her see that video on the tablet?"

"Nope. I want you to keep that one safe, just in case this blows up in my face. That video is the best chance you've got to clear your name if I can't get this done."

"Karen? What are you talking about? If you show that video to Monica Purvis, it's going to be pretty obvious who the killers are, I think."

"I think so, too," Karen said, "but we're talking about some weird kind of corruption, here. While he may not have intended for anyone to die, Lemmons took instructions from someone to commit a crime—physically assaulting those kids—and agreed to do it, even involved other officers. We don't know who that might have been, or how deep the corruption goes, but that means there's a risk even in going to the DA with this. I'm going to call Monica now and tell her what I've got, and find out how soon I can meet with her. All I need you to do is stay completely out of sight somewhere until I call."

Sam opened his mouth twice with no sound coming out, but finally managed to speak. "Okay," he said. "I've got your back. You just be as careful as you can, okay?"

"Count on it. I'll be in touch as soon as I know something good."

The phone went dead in his ear and Sam put it back into his pocket. He made a couple more turns to randomize his route, but his mind wouldn't stop wrestling with the situation. Now that Karen had mentioned the possibility that high-level corruption might be involved, the whole case was taking on even more ominous overtones.

Karen had been correct. The first crime involved in this whole mess had been Lemmons's agreement to rough up those kids and frighten the girl. In fact, just knowing that someone wanted it done quietly made it worse; there were numerous legitimate ways to deal with rebellious teenagers, but somebody hadn't wanted whatever issues she had to be made public. Maybe that was just a family afraid of public scorn, but what if there was something going on with the girl that needed to be covered up? What if the kid was suffering some kind of abuse and was acting out because she didn't feel safe at home?

All of these thoughts built up into a frustration that finally boiled over. There was one person he could think of who had the power to recruit someone like Lemmons, and he decided it was time to take the bull by the horns.

He took out his phone again and dialed his wife's number. Indie answered on the first ring. "Sam?"

"It's me," he said. "Baby, things are getting a little hairy. I need you to look up a number for me, okay?"

"What do you mean, hairy? What's going on, Sam?"

"Jerry Lemmons is dead. He was shot and killed by another cop, and I'm pretty sure they had planned on killing me at the same time but I got away. Lemmons admitted he's got Tracy stashed somewhere, and I was trying to negotiate her release with him when he was killed. The problem is that there's somebody else involved, and I don't know who it is yet. The killings were an accident, Lemmons and his crew were supposed to just rough the kids up and scare the girl into straightening up her act, but she ended up dead. They killed the two boys with her just to cover everything up, but the whole thing is unraveling. I need to find out who recruited them for this, because it may well have been somebody powerful in local government. Karen Parks has a copy of the video and is taking it to the DA right now, but that means she's sticking her neck out. If the wrong people want this covered up, she could be in just as much danger as I am."

"Oh, my God," Indie said. "Whose number do you need me to find?"

"Randy Whitaker," Sam said, "the city attorney. But I don't want his office number, I want his cell."

"I know who you mean," she replied. "He's the one who was mixed up with Candy's ex-husband. Hang on a minute, my computer is right here." Sam heard her set the phone down and then he could hear the clicking of keys on her laptop. A moment later, she returned to the line. "I'll text you the number," she said. "Sam—Sam, just be careful."

"Ain't I always? I love you. Give Kenzie a kiss for me. Hopefully, this will all be over soon and you guys can come home."

He ended the call, but his phone beeped a moment later when the text message came in. He looked at it and then punched the number into the dial pad.

"Hello?" Whitaker said as he answered.

"Remember you promised me a couple of favors?" Sam asked. "I need to collect on one of them."

"I promised you what? Oh—Prichard?"

"Yes. I need to know if you were involved in something, and I need a straight answer."

"Okay, shoot. If there is one man in the world I won't lie to, it'll be you."

"Couple of weeks back, Detective Jerry Lemmons was approached by someone about doing a 'scared straight' bit on a young girl, and he was promised what he called career enhancements if he pulled it off. I don't remember the name, but she was from an influential family and was running the streets with a couple of punk boys. Shortly after that, she disappeared and it was all over the news. Was it you who recruited Lemmons for that job?"

"No," Whitaker said. "Think about everything you know about me, and you should realize I don't involve the police in any of my activities. If someone had come to me with this, I would have sent someone a lot scarier than a cop to have a talk with the kid."

Sam mulled over what Whitaker had said and concluded that he was probably telling the truth. "Okay," he said, "I believe you. So, tell me this: who else is out there that might have made Lemmons an offer like that?"

"Hell, I don't know. If we're talking about the girl who disappeared a couple weeks ago, I can tell you that her grandfather wields a lot of power, but I doubt he'd go straight to the police himself. He's a lawyer, his name is James Wilfrid Weintraub. My guess, if he wanted cops to do something like this, he'd either go to the DA or somebody big at the police department."

"Weintraub," Sam said. "Thank you. Got a number for him?"

"Hang on a second," Whitaker said. A moment later he recited a number that Sam committed to memory.

Sam ended the call and then immediately dialed Weintraub's number. The phone rang three times before it was answered by a secretary.

"Morris, Weintraub and Gill," she said. "How may I direct your call?"

"I need to speak to Mr. Weintraub, please," Sam said. "My name is Sam Prichard."

"One moment." Classical music began to play, and a moment later a gruff voice came on the line.

"This is Jim Weintraub. Mr. Prichard? How can I help you?"

"Mr. Weintraub, I'm a private investigator. In the course of my current investigation, I've come across information regarding your granddaughter, the one who's missing."

"Alyssa? Do you know where she is?"

"Not exactly," Sam said. "Mr. Weintraub, it's my understanding that you asked someone to arrange for her to be scared by police officers. Is that correct?"

The old man hesitated for a moment. "I think there

may have been a conversation along that line," he said cautiously. "What do you know about my granddaughter?"

"Mr. Weintraub, I need to know who you approached about that. It's very important, sir."

Another hesitation. "First, tell me what you know about my granddaughter. Where is Alyssa?"

Sam let out a sigh. "Mr. Weintraub, I'm sorry to tell you that your granddaughter is dead. It was during the attempt to scare her straight, one of the police officers involved accidentally strangled her. He and other officers then killed two boys that were with her, and their bodies were disposed of. I don't know where at this point. I'm trying to bring those officers to justice, but I need to know who you spoke to that recruited them to do this."

There was a strangled cry on the other end of the line, and then Sam could hear muffled sobs. It took almost a minute for the old man to compose himself enough to come back onto the phone. "Mr. Prichard, are you certain she's dead? Is there any chance…"

"Sir, I'm sorry, but there's no doubt. By a strange stroke of fate, there was actually a video camera that recorded the whole thing. I've seen the video, and there's no doubt that she is dead."

Somehow, the old man managed to hold himself together. "Can you assure me that the officers responsible are going to pay?"

"That's what I'm trying to accomplish right now, sir. That's why I need the name. I need to be certain that we don't run afoul of someone who can cover this up."

The old man took a deep breath. "One of my firm's former associate attorneys works for the District Attorney's office," he said. "We were having lunch together, discussing a case she was prosecuting when the subject of my granddaughter came up. She told me she knew of a way to make Alyssa straighten up but that it would cost, and I said I didn't care what it cost me. I gave her 100,000 dollars, which she said would be passed on to those who would actually do the job."

She? Sam thought, and a chill ran down his spine. "Sir, the name?"

"It was Monica Purvis, Mr. Prichard," the old man said, "and I will pay you three times that amount if you can include her in the charges you are pursuing against the officers."

"That won't be necessary, sir," Sam said, and hit the button that ended the call. He dialed Karen's number with his thumb, and listened to the ringing of the phone in his ear.

After six rings, it went to voicemail, and Sam pointed the truck downtown.

* * * * *

He hadn't heard any sign of pursuit in quite some time, but he was sure they'd never give up completely.

There was no telling how long he'd been running through these woods, but every step had made him angrier and angrier. They were treating him like a criminal, but he wasn't the one who had murdered three teenagers.

Marty had been avoiding roads and houses, but now he was getting tired. When a big house suddenly loomed ahead of him, he started to think about asking someone, anyone, for help. After listening for several minutes and hearing nothing, he carefully made his way to the back door of the place and knocked.

There was no answer, and Marty felt a despair start to set in. It was almost like he was the last man on the planet, out here all alone, and he was feeling desperate in ways he'd never experienced before. He was a hunted man, Tracy was still missing and God only knew if she was alive, and suddenly it was all too much.

He went off the porch and found a rock, then threw it through the glass on the door. A moment later, he reached in and unlocked it, then walked inside slowly. If anyone was there, they hadn't reacted to the crash.

A few minutes later, Marty knew he was all alone.

He looked through the kitchen and found some crackers and cookies, enough to at least curb the hunger that was starting to hurt, then washed them down with water from the tap. It was cold and good, and he started to feel just a little better. Refreshed, he began looking around again and found a phone hanging on the kitchen wall.

He grabbed it up, but there was no dial tone. This was apparently a vacation retreat, and the owner didn't leave the phone on when he wasn't present. He hung it up and explored the house further, and that's when he saw the desk.

He yanked open a drawer and looked through it, not sure what he was hoping to find, but was surprised when he saw the Colt .38 revolver. He picked up the gun and saw that it was loaded, then stuffed it into his waistband.

He found a ring of keys in another drawer and noticed that there were car keys on it. A quick glance through the windows showed him a Chevy four-wheel drive pickup, and when he tried the key, it fired right up.

He had wheels, and he had a gun. It was time to stop being the hunted and become the hunter. He put the truck into gear and started down the mountain.

14

Monica Purvis was sitting in her office when Karen called, and listened intently to the story Karen told. "So, this whole thing was recorded on video?"

"Yes," Karen said. "I have a copy of that video that I need to show you, but Sam and I are pretty sure a couple of these cops have already gone rogue. You heard about Jerry Lemmons being killed?"

"Yes, just a few minutes ago," Monica said, "but the story I got is that your friend Prichard killed him. We've got two officers who witnessed it."

"Yeah, yeah, Driscoll and Slocum. Those two have starring roles in the video I'm going to show you. Driscoll is the one who actually killed the girl, and then the rest of them worked together to kill the two boys. Lemmons had just told Sam he'd give up those two and let them take the fall for the murder when he was shot. Pretty safe bet they heard it and decided to shut him up while they could, wouldn't you think?"

Monica made a snap decision. "Okay, look, it's eleven thirty right now, and I've got to meet with my boss in ten minutes. I'll go over this with her, but you be here at twelve and bring me that video. I'll go ahead and get started on the paperwork by then. You said it's Driscoll, Slocum, Forsyth and Wright?"

"That's them, yeah. I'll be there at one o'clock."

"Okay," Monica said. "And listen, don't let anybody else know about this yet. With dirty cops involved, you have to be careful. I'll see you then." She hung up the phone and stared at it for a moment, then picked it up and dialed another number.

"Precinct 3, Sergeant McLean."

"Sergeant, this is Assistant District Attorney Monica Purvis. Are officers Forsyth and Wright on duty?"

"Yes, ma'am," the sergeant said. "They're on patrol. Would you like to speak to their supervisor?"

"Yes, please." He was placed on hold for a moment, and then another man picked up the line.

"Lieutenant Stevens, how can I help you?"

"Lieutenant Stevens, this is Assistant District Attorney Monica Purvis. Would it be possible for me to borrow a couple of your officers for a special assignment? I'm talking about Officers Forsyth and Wright."

"Just one moment," the lieutenant said. "Yes,

ma'am, they're both on duty right now. Shall I have them call you?"

"Yes, have one of them call Monica Purvis at the DA's office as soon as possible, and thank you."

She hung up the phone again and leaned back in her chair to wait. A moment later, it rang again and she snatched it up. "Purvis."

"Ms. Purvis? This is David Forsyth, I was told to call you immediately?"

"And it's a damned good thing you did," Monica said. "Remember that mess about those kids a couple weeks ago? Did you know it was freaking caught on video?"

The cop on the line stuttered for a moment, but she cut him off. "Don't even bother trying to deny anything," she said. "Karen Parks has a copy of that damned video, and she's bringing it to me at noon. I need you here when she arrives, we've got to make sure no one ever sees that damned thing."

Forsyth seemed shocked. "Make sure what? I don't..."

"Who the hell do you think handed you guys that job? Those kids are dead, Jerry Lemmons is dead...If it gets out that I set this mess up, I'm going down with you, so right now I'm your guardian angel. Where's your partner?"

"He's right here with me," he said. "Why..."

"You get your ass up here to wait for Parks, and send him to go and find James Weintraub. It's lunchtime, so he'll be at Marconi's. Tell Wright to say he found Weintraub's granddaughter and needs to take him to her, and he'll go along. And tell him to make sure his body won't be found anytime soon."

It took Forsyth a moment to regain his voice. "Ma'am," he said, "you want us to kill them? Karen's a fellow cop, and Weintraub's a pretty big man..."

"You want us all to go down for murdering those kids and Lemmons and God knows who else? These people know just enough to make that happen, so you're going to get a little more blood on your hands, got that? And once you've got Karen Parks, you can use her to get Sam Prichard, because that bastard has the original video. You've got to find him, too, and then shut all of them up for good."

There was muffled whispering, and then Forsyth came back on the line. "Um...All right, we're in. I'll— I'll be there shortly." He hung up, and Monica slammed the phone back into the cradle once more.

Forsyth's partner, Mark Wright, was driving their patrol car, so he dropped Forsyth off about ten minutes later. The cop looked around for a moment, then spotted some bushes in front of the building and went to stand behind them. He knew Karen Parks, and the thought of doing her any harm was making his stomach churn, but he also knew what happened to cops who went to prison.

Karen pulled in a few minutes before noon and eased the car into an empty parking slot near the front of the building. She dropped the keys into her purse and started to get out, but suddenly the front passenger door was yanked open and she looked around to see who was getting in.

It was David Forsyth, and he had his service automatic in his hand. "Just sit down, Karen," he said nervously. "Get back behind the wheel and start the car."

Karen stared at the gun for a moment, then pulled the door shut. "Dave, hasn't this already gone far enough?"

"Start the car, Karen," he said. "We're just going for a little ride. All I want is the videos you and Prichard have, and then you can go home. Just start the car and let's go out towards Arvada for the moment." He kept the gun aimed at her head as he reached across her and took her own pistol out of the holster she kept clipped to her belt.

She carefully reached into her purse for the keys, but then looked up at him again as she inserted them into the ignition. "Monica Purvis already knows," she said. "She's expecting me any second."

"Who do you think called me?" Forsyth asked. "What, did you think I stumbled across you out of luck? Now let's go. Start the car and put it in gear."

Realization dawned on her, and she started the car. She backed out of the parking space and drove out onto the street, turning in the general direction of Aurora. "So, is this it? Are you going to kill me?"

"Hell, no! That's what I was told to do, but all I want is the videos. You give me those, and drop all this, and no one will ever believe it existed. You and Prichard let this go, and it's all over."

Karen swallowed once and indicated her purse with a nod of her head. "It's on my phone," she said. "Right there in my purse, you can take it now."

He glanced into her purse on the seat and saw the phone sticking out of it. Keeping the gun trained on her, he reached in and picked it up. "Okay, that's half the problem. Now, let's go find your buddy Prichard. I understand he has a copy of it, too."

Karen's heart sank, but she tried to keep it from showing on her face. "Sam Prichard? I don't know where he is, I haven't talked to him in weeks."

Forsyth laughed. "Don't play games, Karen," he said. "You must've told Monica about him, because she said I got to get one from him, too."

The phone in his hand suddenly began to ring, and it startled him. His eyes went to the phone for a split second, but then he raised them back up to watch Karen as he turned the phone to let her see the display. "Is that him?"

Karen glanced at the number and saw that it was

Sam's throwaway, but she shook her head in the negative. "I don't know who that is," she said. "I ignore calls from numbers I don't know."

The ringing continued for a moment, then stopped. Forsyth called up the phone app and looked at its recent calls. "That's funny," he said, "the same number shows up several times today." He poked her arm with the barrel of the gun. "It's Prichard, isn't it?"

"I told you, I don't know who that is. Probably one of those sales calls, I get those all the time."

Forsyth watched her for a moment, then grinned. "You're sweating, Karen," he said. "Awful lot of stress in your voice. Tell you what, I'm going to call that number back and put it on speaker. If it's Sam, you tell him you need to meet up. Tell him to meet you at that old appliance factory out on Jamison, in Arvada."

Karen looked at him for a second and then cut her eyes back to the road. "And if I don't?"

"Look, all I want is the videos, but I have to get them. If you don't do what I tell you, or you try to warn him in any way, I'm gonna do what I have to do. You got kids, Karen, don't you want to go home to them tonight?"

Karen swallowed hard and looked at Forsyth again. "Yeah," she said softly. "I do."

Forsyth nodded, then hit the call-back icon. On speaker, the phone rang only once before Sam answered.

"Karen, don't go to Monica! I just found out she's the one who set this all up with Lemmons."

"Yeah, I know," Karen said, "I found that out, too. Sam, we need to meet up. You know that old factory in Arvada, where they used to make refrigerators? How soon can you get there?"

"I know the place. I'm probably thirty minutes away."

Karen glanced at Forsyth. "Okay, so am I. I'll see you there, and we can talk this over and decide what to do."

"I'll be there," Sam said, and then he was gone.

Forsyth grinned. "See, that wasn't so hard. Relax, Karen, this will all be over soon."

* * * * *

James Wilfrid Weintraub was a creature of habit. When he had hung up the phone from talking to Sam, he had sat at his desk for only a few moments before rising and heading for the door. Twice each week he had lunch at Marconi's, and this was one of those days. Letting his body operate on autopilot allowed him to think about what Prichard had told him, and he was already out on the sidewalk in front of his building before he even realized it. His feet carried him three doors down and turned into the restaurant without even consulting his conscious mind.

The maître d' smiled at him and led the way to the table he always used. A waiter set the customary chilled water glass in front of him and handed him a menu. Weintraub waived it away and ordered the veal that he loved without thinking.

Alyssa was dead. That thought kept rolling over and over, and though he wanted to reject it with every fiber of his being, the fact that she had not been seen in more than two weeks just seemed to confirm it. He let his memory show him a collage of images from his granddaughter's life, from when she was just a newborn to the last time he'd seen her almost three weeks earlier.

She was a beautiful girl, and so full of promise for the future. His daughter had been so proud when Alyssa was born, so proud to show the baby off to her grandpa, and Weintraub had lavished gifts on the child since that day. She was his precious little angel, he'd always thought, and it was to him she would run when that lousy father of hers would go into one of his moods.

George Russell, Alyssa's father, had seemed like a fine young man when he had become Weintraub's son-in-law. He was a dentist who had recently opened his own practice and seemed to be doing well. For the first few years, George was nothing but a blessing to the family, but then Alyssa was born. For most men, having a child will cause them to suddenly take life more seriously. For George, it seemed to represent only a greater burden.

The doctors said George had always suffered from depression, but he had managed to keep it under control for most of his life. It wasn't until he became a father that it really became obvious and began to affect those around him. When Alyssa was a baby, he would occasionally slip into a funk and begin to worry about things that shouldn't have been any kind of serious issue, but as she grew, his depression got worse.

By the time she was ten years old, George's depression reached the point that it was interfering with every aspect of his life. His wife and daughter had given up trying to reach him during those periods, and were avoiding him as much as they could. His dental practice began to suffer due to constant rescheduling of appointments, and it wasn't long before even his most loyal patients were going elsewhere. Weintraub had convinced him to take on a couple of other young dentists, and limit himself to a managerial capacity. That, at least, preserved the family's income.

In the last couple of years, however, George had started to become belligerent during his episodes. The slightest insult could set him off, and he would often go into a verbal rage that would last for hours. The whole thing had come to a head six months earlier, when George had grown angry at Alyssa for closing her bedroom door while he was talking to her, and literally kicked it down.

Weintraub had pulled strings to get George into a hospital in California, a place that was known for its treatment of depression and anger issues, but with sufficient discretion to keep the treatment from ever becoming publicly known. George had spent three months there, and seemed to be doing better when he got home.

Unfortunately, his anger and belligerence had already taken their toll on Alyssa. During his absence, she had begun acting out, getting into minor trouble and running with kids who demonstrated a lack of respect for authority. She had begun to display a similar attitude, even to her grandfather.

It was during lunch at Marconi's that he finally opened up about the issue to someone he thought he could trust. Monica Purvis had been a rising star in his law firm, but she had become disillusioned after successfully defending a man who had been charged with the rape and murder of a young woman. Her duty as an attorney was to provide the best defense she possibly could, and she had done that duty despite the fact that she was personally certain of his guilt.

A month later, she had tendered her resignation from the firm and accepted a position with the Denver District Attorney's office. She and Weintraub had remained friends, and often met for lunch to discuss cases before facing each other in court.

They had also become lovers, carrying on an occasional affair that had already lasted more than two years. That was why Weintraub had confided in her; he felt that she could be trusted, and that she genuinely cared about him and his family.

And now he had to face the fact that that confidence had led to the death of the granddaughter he loved more than anyone or anything else in the world. Tears were slowly running down his cheeks as he waited for his lunch to be delivered, but then a motion to his left caught his eye.

A police officer was approaching his table, directed by the maître d'. Weintraub looked up, and his heart began pounding as he wondered if this officer was bringing him the official news of Alyssa's death. The look on the officer's face was grim, reinforcing Weintraub's assumption, but he never got to hear the words themselves.

James Wilfrid Weintraub blinked furiously several times, and then both hands went to his chest. A strangled cry came from his mouth as he pitched forward, and then his final breath exited with a rattling sound.

He had never told anyone what his doctor had said only a few weeks before. He had never shared the fact that his heart was enlarged and exhibiting signs of congestive failure.

He hadn't even told Monica.

A few people screamed, and paramedics were called immediately. They worked on the old man for a few minutes, but it was quickly apparent that he was gone. A patrol officer who happened to be present when

Weintraub collapsed watched long enough to be sure there was no hope, then turned and hurried out the door.

When he was away from the restaurant, he took out a cell phone and dialed a number. "It's Wright," he said. "Talk about a stroke of luck. The lawyer, Weintraub? He just keeled over of a heart attack, he's dead."

On the other end of the call, Forsyth shook his head as he watched Karen pull into the parking lot. "Somehow, I don't think my end of this is going to be that easy. I'll call you once I'm done, okay?"

"Yeah," Wright said. "Let me know where to pick you up when it's over."

15

Sam hung up the phone and took the next left turn. Arvada was off to the north, and Jamison was on the west end of town. Hopefully, he and Karen could figure out a next move that would bring this mess to a conclusion.

Sam glanced at the clock on the truck's fancy radio and saw that it was already ten minutes after one. He had expected some sort of announcement by the police regarding the murder of Marty Fletcher to be released around noon, so he turned on the radio and tuned it to the local all-news station.

The first two stories he heard were about the antics of the new president and a celebrity who had passed away. The third story began, but was suddenly interrupted by the ominous music that always accompanied a breaking news announcement.

"We interrupt our regularly scheduled news

broadcast to announce the sudden passing of prominent Denver attorney James Wilfrid Weintraub. Mr. Weintraub collapsed only minutes ago at Marconi's restaurant, where he had just ordered lunch. Witnesses said he was apparently clutching his chest, and paramedics on the scene believe he may have suffered a massive coronary. We'll bring you more information as it becomes available."

Sam was so stunned he had to pull the truck over. He had spoken to Weintraub less than twenty minutes earlier, giving him the terrible news of the death of his granddaughter. Apparently it was too much for the old man to handle.

There wasn't time to worry about it, though, so after a couple of minutes he put the truck back in gear and continued on toward the old factory. The frustrating thing was that, without Weintraub, it might not be possible to implicate Monica Purvis. Sam would have to wait and find out how Karen learned of her involvement, but bringing her to justice might have to wait for another time.

The Rayburn Appliance company had gone out of business nearly 8 years earlier, and a couple of their facilities in other locations had been bought up by some of their competitors. Their factory in Denver, however, was the oldest one they'd had and was already in poor condition when the company folded. As a result, it had sat empty all this time.

The police made occasional sweeps of the building, rounding up or running off the homeless and drug dealers who tried to use it as shelter. Normally, they would have left the homeless alone, but the building was so bad that it was considered unsafe. Two sections had collapsed already, and a couple of old veterans had lost their lives. The city tried to keep it boarded up, but some people always found a way to get inside.

The big parking lot was occasionally used for car shows, swap meets and as a hangout for kids at night, but during weekdays it was usually abandoned. When it came into view, Sam saw Karen's car sitting far toward the back and gave the truck some throttle as he headed toward it. He pulled up with her on his left, and leaned out the window as he put the truck in park and shut off the engine.

"Got here as fast as I could," he said. "I gotta tell you, I was scared to death when I found out Monica was involved. How did you—"

A sudden movement caught his eye as David Forsyth rose from where he'd been crouched on the other side of Karen's car. He had a gun in his right hand, and Sam was staring down the barrel.

"Hey, Sam," Forsyth said. "Sorry we have to meet again under conditions like these, but I need you to keep your hands where I can see them and step out of the truck."

Sam thought about going for his own gun, but then

he saw that Forsyth had another pistol in his left, and that it was pointed through the window at Karen. If he made a move, Karen was certain to be shot. He held his hands out the window and used the outside door handle to pop it open.

"Hey, Dave," he said as he stepped out onto the concrete. "What's this all about?"

"Give it up, Sam. I've already got Karen's copy of the video, now I just need yours. You hand it over and this can all end peacefully."

Still keeping his hands visible, Sam grinned at him. "I don't think so," he said. "Once I let Karen make a copy, I figured keeping that video with me might be a mistake. It's stashed away somewhere safe, and if anything happens to either of us I can guarantee it will go straight to the FBI."

Forsyth's face suddenly went sour, and he tightened his grip on the gun aimed at Sam. "Now, that was stupid, Sam," he said. "Aren't you already in enough trouble? I hear they're looking for you on a couple of different murder charges at the moment, right? If you'd just hand that video over, you might have a chance to get away. I'm sure not going to try and take you in, and I know Karen won't. How about you come over and get into the car, and tell Karen where it is. She can drive us there and let you fetch it, and then you guys can drop me off and go your merry way."

When a man has a gun pointed at you and you're

certain he's willing to use it, the only thing you can do is try to keep him calm and look for an opening. Sam bit his bottom lip as if thinking it over, then shrugged his shoulders. "And if I do, you'll let us go? No sudden bullets in the back of the head?"

"You have my word," Forsyth said. "Let's face it, Sam, without the video there's nothing you can do to tie us to what happened. You can talk all you want, but it'll be your word against four cops, so it's not likely anyone's going to believe you. Hell, especially when you're already wanted for murder. You give me that video, Karen can go on with her life and you can get back in that truck and head for Canada, for all I care."

Sam shrugged again. "What about Tracy Jensen? I tried to give the video to Jerry Lemmons, to get her back. Will you let her go?"

Forsyth looked confused. "Who the hell is she? I don't know any Tracy Jensen."

Sam's heart sank. "She was working with the guy who made the video, trying to work it out with Lemmons so nobody else would get hurt. She disappeared a few days ago, and I'm pretty sure Lemmons has her locked away somewhere. Any idea where that might be?"

It was Forsyth's turn to shrug his shoulders. "I'm afraid not, old buddy. Tell you what, though, let's take care of our business, and then I'll see what I can find out."

Sam looked him in the eye for another moment, then nodded slowly. He walked carefully around the front of Karen's car, then turned his back when Forsyth ordered him to do so. A moment later, he felt his Glock lifted from its holster and Forsyth told him to climb into the front seat.

Sam opened the door and got in as Forsyth slid into the backseat. The car was an unmarked, which meant there was no divider between the front and back seat. With three guns, Forsyth could easily kill either or both of them whenever he chose.

"Okay, now tell her where to go," Forsyth said.

Sam looked over at Karen, who gave him a rueful smile. "It's at my friend Harry's place in Northglenn," he said. "Jump on I-25 and head north, I'll tell you where to get off."

Karen started the car and left the parking lot, then turned right onto West 52nd Avenue. She followed it for a mile and then merged onto Interstate 76, which would lead to I-25.

Sam turned his head enough to look into the backseat. "Dave," he said, "you know I saw the video. It was pretty obvious to me you didn't really want to be involved in that whole thing, so how about you change sides and help us do this the right way? It was Driscoll and Slocum and Lemmons who were really to blame for all this. Lemmons is already dead, but he had the idea of letting Driscoll and Slocum take the heat. We

160

could still do that."

"Yeah? And how would that work?"

"Simple enough," Sam said. "We forget about the videos completely. Lemmons said Driscoll and Slocum killed all three of the kids, and then blackmailed the rest of you into helping to cover it up by threatening to claim you were involved. If you back up my statement that one of them heard Lemmons giving me his confession, that's enough motive for them to kill him, and would get me off that hook. As for Fletcher, I'd say we could probably find some evidence that Lemmons sent them out to get him, too. You and Wright just admit that Lemmons ordered you to go along, but now you want to come clean. If the four of us stick together on it, it can work."

Forsyth was watching him as he spoke, but Sam could read his face. The man wasn't going for it.

"Trouble with that, Sam," Forsyth said, "is that I don't trust you not to change your story at the last minute. The way it is now, you give me that video and no one is ever going to believe anything you two say about it, anyway. I think we're going to stick to my plan. You give me the video, and then you hightail it out of town. Karen here is smart, she's not going to talk about this at all, are you, Karen?"

Karen didn't answer, so Forsyth poked the back of her head with a gun barrel. She flinched, then said, "I won't say a word." She flicked her eyes in Sam's direction, and he could see just how frightened she really was in that glance.

Sam turned back to face the windshield, his mind racing. He didn't believe for a second that Forsyth was going to let them go; despite what he was saying, both Sam and Karen had sterling reputations, and it was unlikely their statements would go unheeded. If both of them told the same story, there was a very good chance the FBI would launch an investigation, and sooner or later one of the four dirty cops would crack under questioning. The only hope they had was to eliminate everyone who might know the truth, and he was certain that was what Forsyth had been told.

The only question was whether the man was actually capable of murder. Sam wasn't sure, but he didn't think Forsyth had ever fired his gun in the line of duty, and he kept thinking about the way he had reacted when the girl had died. He was the only one there who had wanted to try to save her, so there was a chance...

The car merged onto the northbound interstate, meaning that Sam had maybe another twenty minutes to come up with a miracle. He thought of Lemmons's pistol, still tucked into the glove box of the truck, and suddenly wished he had stuffed it into his sock.

Might as well wish for Bruce Lee to come to my rescue, Sam thought. *Damn thing wouldn't have stayed in my sock, anyway.*

Sam's old friend Harry Winslow really did have a

house in Northglenn, but Sam didn't have a key to it. It had been locked up since Harry got his big promotion and moved off to DC, but there was another destination in Northglenn that Sam had in mind.

Harry had once been the Denver station chief for the Department of Homeland Security. That was before DHS genuinely considered Denver a potential terrorist hotbed, but Sam had been instrumental in breaking up a terrorist cell that operated from there a little over a year before. Back then, Harry's entire office consisted of a couple of guys who were essentially just a pair of computer hackers, operating out of a rundown building in the back streets of the suburb.

When Harry's budget for the office was increased after that near disaster, he had gotten a nicer place downtown, but he had kept Ron Thomas and Jeff Donaldson in the same location they had used for three years. And then, when Harry had gotten the big promotion and moved up to DHS headquarters in DC, Ron and Jeff had decided it was time to enter the private sector. Still operating from the same building, they now hired their services out to clients all over the world who had a lawful use for them. Their specialties were network security and industrial and corporate counterespionage, and they were very good at both.

Sam knew them both to be extremely intelligent and resourceful, and he'd been known to drop by and say hello once in a while. They always welcomed him, and often asked if he might need their help someday.

It seemed to Sam that day had finally arrived. When they got off the interstate, Sam directed Karen toward the old building. She parked in front of its only door a few minutes later, and Sam turned to look at Forsyth.

"My buddy Harry runs this place," he said, "and I left the tablet with one of his employees. All I'm going to do is get out of the car and knock on the door. I'll tell them I need it, and they'll get it for me. Soon as they do, I'll come straight back."

Forsyth nodded. "Be sure you do," he said, "because Karen is going to stay here and keep me company. I'm sure you don't want anything to happen to her, now do you?"

"Like I said," Sam said, "I'll get it and come right back. You can watch me the whole time, I won't even step inside."

Forsyth nodded again, and Sam stepped out of the car. He walked up to the battered old door and knocked three times, then twice more.

A thin young man who was already losing his hair opened the door and smiled at him. Sam winked once, and saw Ron Thomas throw a split-second glance at the car.

"Hey, Sam," Ron said.

"Hey, Ron. Listen, remember that tablet I dropped off a while ago? Sorry to be a pain in the butt, but I need it back. Can you grab it for me?" Sam hadn't dropped off anything, of course, so the ruse instantly told Ron that Sam was in trouble.

Ron grinned. "Sure, no problem. I put it on my workbench, give me just a minute." He turned around, leaving the door open, and disappeared from view. He was gone about a minute, then returned and handed Sam an iPad. "Here you go," he said. "Anything else I can do for you?"

Sam glanced over Ron's shoulder and saw Jeff Donaldson and another man he didn't recognize. Both of them were holding submachine guns. "Nope," Sam said. "I think that's it. Thanks a lot, and I'll see you later."

Sam turned and started to step toward the car, but Ron leaned out. "Hey, is that your wife? Tell her I said hi." He waved and gave a silly grin toward Karen, who smiled and waved back.

Sam laughed and continued toward the car. He opened the door and slid inside, noticing that Ron was still standing in the open doorway. He waved back at the young man, then turned and handed the tablet to Forsyth.

It came off like precision clockwork. Forsyth lowered his eyes for only a couple of seconds to look at the tablet, as Ron jerked back inside the door out of the way. Donaldson and the other man exploded out the door, their guns pointed directly at Forsyth as they both started yelling at him to drop his weapons and raise his hands.

Forsyth had put down the pistol in his right hand when he took the tablet from Sam, but the other one was still pressed against the back of Karen's seat. He looked up in shocked surprise at the two men aiming machine guns at him, and Sam twisted suddenly and grabbed Karen, dragging her across the seat and onto himself.

Forsyth squeezed the trigger in reflex, and the bullet passed through the seat, creasing Karen's left buttock before lodging in the dashboard. He stared at the machine guns that were pointed at his face, then quickly dropped the gun and raised both hands.

Ron stepped out calmly and walked over to open the back door of the car. "Would you mind stepping out of the vehicle, sir? We get really upset when people point guns at our friends."

16

With a pair of wicked-looking automatic rifles pointed at him, Forsyth carefully got out of the car. Sam retrieved his Glock and passed Karen's gun back to her, then gave her Forsyth's pistol, as well. Karen was sitting on her right cheek, pressing a sanitary napkin to the gouge in her butt.

"Damn, Sam," she said shrilly, "this freaking hurts!"

Ron and Sam each took one of her arms and helped her walk into the building, while Jeff and the other man, whose name was Mike, escorted Forsyth. They marched him into a room that was set up as a holding cell and locked him inside, then Jeff brought a first aid kit into the break room, where Karen was now seated on the couch.

"If you think I'm dropping my pants with you guys in here," Karen yelled, "you can all think again. Give me the damn first aid kit and get out!"

They got. The four men stepped out into the hallway, and Mike unlocked the holding cell door and opened it. Sam stood in the doorway and looked at Forsyth, who was sitting on a bunk mounted to the wall and simply staring at the floor. A glance over his shoulder told him Karen had left the day room door partly open, and could hear everything clearly.

He turned to Forsyth again. "It's all over for you, Dave," Sam said. "There are only two ways you can help yourself, right now. One is to roll over and turn state's evidence against the others, and the second is to help me find Tracy Jensen."

Forsyth looked up at him. "I told you," he said, "I have no idea who she is or where she is. If Lemmons did something with her, I never heard about it."

Sam stood there in silence for a few seconds, then shook his head. "Then you'd better hope we find her alive some other way, or you're going to be looking at yet another murder charge. If she dies, I'll see to it that all of you are charged. Understand me?"

Forsyth spread his arms wide. "Look, Sam, this whole thing got out of control, I admit it. You want me to roll on the others? I will, no problem. But when I tell you I don't know who this woman is, I'm telling you the truth. Believe me, right now I wish I did know where she was. Helping you find her might give me a shot at staying out of prison."

"Then think, man. Where would Lemmons put someone he wanted to keep on ice, but keep alive? I still think she might be okay, because Lemmons was talking about letting her go. Can you come up with any idea where I might look?"

Forsyth looked at the floor again, but after a moment he shook his head. "I wasn't close to Lemmons," he said, "not like Driscoll. They were tight, really tight. Driscoll and his partner were the regular muscle Jerry used. Hell, they were into a lot of things you don't even know about. Drug shakedowns, robbing dealers—after that mess with those kids, Wright and I got brought into it, and it wasn't like we were given a choice. I even heard Driscoll say once that they had a fantastic place to get rid of bodies, but I never asked where it was."

Sam stared at him for another minute, thinking. "What about your partner? Was he involved in these things?"

Forsyth shook his head. "No way," he said, "up until this, he and I were both pretty clean. Hell, we weren't even supposed to be there that night. We were driving by and saw something going on, and just stopped out of curiosity." He looked up at Sam and grinned. "Purvis, she told me to take you two out and kill you, but I couldn't have done it. When Mark killed that boy, it was all I could do not to start crying. I wanted to run, I wanted to stop it somehow, but I—I was scared. If I hadn't gone along with it all, I think they would've killed me." He lowered his eyes again. "I couldn't have killed you guys. I really was gonna let you go."

Sam thought about what he'd seen on the video. Other than watching, Forsyth had not actively participated in the murders, and it was possible he was telling the truth. Unfortunately, when a wrongful death occurs during the commission of a criminal act, everyone involved is considered to be liable for murder. Good intentions would not be enough to save him.

Appropriate actions, on the other hand, could potentially mitigate the punishment he would receive.

"Dave, the way I see it, you got two choices. You can try to throw yourself on the mercy of the court and hope for the best, or you can work with me and Karen to bring the truly guilty ones to justice. Are you willing to do that?"

Forsyth raised his eyes to Sam's face. "What have you got in mind?"

"I want to bring these children's murderers to justice, and that includes Monica Purvis. In addition, I want to find Tracy Jensen and bring her home safely. There's at least a chance that Slocum or Driscoll might know where she is. If you're willing to help us accomplish that, I think Karen and I could say that you approached us for help. You'd have to claim that you were keeping quiet while you tried to gather evidence against Lemmons and the others, but came to us when Purvis told you about the video. It Karen and I back up that story, you could conceivably get immunity. You might even get to remain a cop."

Forsyth stared at him for a long moment, and then Sam saw tears brim over his eyes and start down his cheeks. "You just tell me what you want me to do, Sam," he said. "I'll do it."

"Wait here a minute," Sam said. He closed the door and turned to Ron. "Could you..."

Ron held up a finger to shush him and motioned for him to follow. They went into another room, with Jeff and Mike trailing along.

"I think I've got a hunch where you're about to go," Ron said, "but I thought we ought to discuss it where he couldn't hear us. You really think you can trust that guy?"

"I've seen people in bad situations before," Sam said. "Sometimes, it's really hard to decide what's the right thing to do, but if you give them a little direction most people will jump at the chance to do the right thing. I saw the video we were talking about, and Dave is right. It was pretty obvious he never meant to be there or in that situation."

"Okay, I can see that, I guess. Still, at the moment you've got at least two murder charges hanging over your head. If I'm understanding what you're planning, you're going to have to turn this guy loose for a while.

What happens if he turns on you?"

Sam's eyes narrowed, just as Karen hobbled into the room. "Actually, I was planning to let Karen take him in. Since he can confirm that an assistant DA is involved and tried to send him to kill us, she's not going to have any trouble walking him straight into the head lady's office. Between him and the video, I'm pretty sure we can close the case."

"Yeah, maybe, but you've still got five loose ends at the moment. There's the other three cops, the assistant DA and the missing woman. If any of the first four twig to what you're doing, you'll never find them, and even if you do, there's no guarantee any of them knows where the lady is or that you'll get to her in time."

Sam cocked his head to one side, glancing quickly at Karen before giving his attention back to Ron. "Okay, you've obviously got something in mind. What is it?"

Ron grinned. "Why don't the two of you play dead? We can fix it up in seconds, and then your boy in there can show pictures of your dead bodies. I can make a copy of the video on a tablet so he's got everything he's supposed to have, and we've got everything we need here to wire him up. With him talking about how he knocked you guys off and even showing proof, the others will think they're in the clear and talk about it. We can get clear, perfect recordings of their conversation, and if we play it right, we might even get the location on the woman who's missing. At least one of them should know where she is, right? The other guy couldn't have done it all alone."

Sam looked at Karen. "What do you think?"

She shrugged. "I heard the deal you offered him, and I agree that he didn't look like he really wanted to be involved. I can go along with your story, but I do want some insurance of some kind. If he wears a wire and can convince them he's all theirs, we can nail all three of the dirty cops and Monica. I'm just not sure he's going to be able to find Tracy for you."

"That's because you're not as devious as we are," Ron said. "What we do here is devise ways to get the information we want. All he's got to do is say that you were going on and on about this Tracy, that you were sure Lemmons had her put away somewhere, and that she's another loose end that has to be tied up. If they know where she is, one or two of them is going to head out to take care of that problem. All we've got to do is follow."

"I don't know," Sam said, "if they spot a tail..."

"They won't. Mikey over there is our resident drone man. He's got some of the neatest little toys you ever saw, little gizmos that can fly along out of sight and follow any target they're given. You and Ms. Karen can ride along with us in the van as we keep track of the drone, and we won't be more than a minute behind it at any time. When they stop, we'll know where she is and can move in."

Sam looked at Karen again, and she shrugged. He crossed his arms and turned back to Ron. "Okay," he said, "let's do it. We just need to move quick."

Ron smiled and turned to look at Jeff. "Jeff! Two fatal head wounds, right now."

The next ten minutes were extremely busy, as Jeff and Ron hurriedly had Sam and Karen climb into the trunk of her car and took pictures, then hurried inside and loaded them into a computer. When it was done, the photos showed gaping wounds in their chests and faces, with blood everywhere. The work was so well done that, even though the pictures were taken from two different angles, the wounds and bloodstains matched perfectly.

Meanwhile, Mike and Sam got Forsyth wired with a highly sensitive microphone and transmitter. Every spoken word within twelve feet would be picked up clearly, though background noises would be eliminated. The signal would be transmitted to a receiver in the van they would be using to follow the drone, so Sam and Karen could hear it all even as it was being recorded.

"We put the pictures onto Karen's phone," Sam told him. "Once they see those, they should be ready to trust you completely. You should tell them it made you sick, since they know you never killed anyone before. If you seem too calm about it, it may look suspicious."

Forsyth nodded. "Oh, don't worry," he said, "they'll

be able to tell I'm upset, because I really am. Those damn pictures made me feel sick, even though I know they aren't real. I think I can pull this off."

"Then all we have to do," Sam said, "is get you together with all of the others. We're going to take you down the street to a convenience store, and you can call for a ride from there. If anyone asks where the bodies are, just say you ditched the car in a parking lot behind one of the apartment complexes. There are a lot of them, so it's believable."

Forsyth agreed, and climbed into a car with Ron. They drove only a few blocks to a convenience store, and Ron let him out. He immediately took his phone from its pouch on his belt and called his partner, Wright.

"I'm all done," he said. "I'm out in Northglenn, the Pick-N-Go at Huron and 116th."

"Nobody saw you?"

"No. I did it out on some farm road out east. Nobody around, nobody saw nothing. Left the car in some parking lot, way back in the back. I don't think anyone will pay attention to it 'til it starts to smell."

Wright was quiet for a moment. "You okay, Dave?"

Forsyth hesitated, his genuine anxiety making him breathe hard into the phone. "I'm okay," he said. "Gotta do what we gotta do, right?"

"Okay. Be there as fast as I can."

Ron had circled the block and parked his car on the street, then climbed into the van with the others. High overhead, one of Mike's drones was hovering, its camera trained on Forsyth. He'd been instructed to remain in plain sight, so he was leaning against a light pole near the corner of the lot.

It took almost 30 minutes for his partner to arrive, and he slid into the car as soon as it pulled up beside him. Mike focused the camera on the top of the car so that it would follow the vehicle, and then they turned their attention to the receiver.

17

"I wasn't sure you had it in you," Wright said. "You're sure it's done, right?"

Forsyth held up Karen's phone and brought up the photo gallery. He tapped on the first photo, showing Sam and Karen lying obviously dead in the trunk of the car, and handed it to his partner. "I hated it," he said, "but I don't want to go to prison, either. I told them I was just going to lock them in the trunk and leave them for someone to find, so they got in." He swallowed hard. "Then I shot 'em."

Wright looked over at him. "Guess you're a little tougher than I thought," he said. "Don't beat yourself up about it, Dave, it had to be done."

"Yeah, but can we stop talking about it? This whole thing makes me kind of sick."

"What about the videos?" Wright asked.

"One's on that phone, and the other is on this iPad."

He held up the tablet Ron had given him. "There aren't any more."

"Okay," Wright said. "That means it's all over, then. Why don't you call Purvis and let her know?"

Forsyth nodded and took out his own phone. He found Monica's number and hit redial.

"District Attorney's Office," the receptionist said. "How may I direct your call?"

"Monica Purvis, please," Forsyth said. The girl put him on hold for a moment, and then Monica answered. "This is Dave Forsyth," he said. "It's all over. We took care of everything, and I've got both the videos."

He could hear her sigh of relief. "That's excellent," she said. "The lawyer is out of the way, too, so I think that wraps it up."

"Okay. Just wanted to let you know." He hung up the phone without even saying goodbye, and then turned to his partner. "We need to meet up with the other two. Prichard kept going on and on about some woman, said Lemmons had her hidden away somewhere. If one of them knows where she is, we need to take care of her, too. That's the last loose end, and we need to make sure there aren't any others."

Right nodded. "Call Driscoll," he said. "Tell him to meet us in the parking lot at Torchy's." Torchy's was a popular Mexican restaurant in downtown Denver.

Forsyth made the call and Driscoll and Slocum agreed to meet them twenty minutes later. High overhead, the little drone flew along with its camera focused on the roof of the car, while the van followed from half a mile behind. When the squad car pulled in at the taco place, Jeff parked the van at a burger joint a block away.

Driscoll and Slocum arrived two minutes later, and the four cops stepped out of their cars and leaned against them. The sensitive microphone Forsyth was wearing picked up the conversation clearly.

"We think it's all about over," Wright said. "Monica Purvis, the assistant DA, she called us a while ago and told Dave to deal with Karen Parks and Sam Prichard, while I took care of that old lawyer, Weintraub. I got lucky and the old fart dropped dead of a heart attack before I could get to him, but Dave took care of Karen and Sam the hard way." He handed over Karen's phone so the other two could see the photo of their bodies.

Slocum let out a low whistle. "Way to go, Dave," he said. "So, that gets rid of everybody who knew anything?"

"Not quite," Forsyth said. "Prichard was talking about some woman that knew about the video, and he thinks Lemmons had her locked up somewhere. I don't know anything about it and neither does Mark, we're hoping you do."

Driscoll scowled. "Yeah, I know who you mean. She was trying to work with Fletcher to hang us all. Jerry stashed her in someplace in Lakewood. The way he talked, she knows everything. I guess we better get rid of her, too."

"Do you know where she is? We don't."

"Yeah, I know where. It's a place we use now and then when we need to hide something."

Forsyth nodded. "Okay, we'll let you guys do that. You already took care of the guy who made the video, right?"

Slocum made a grimace. "Well, actually...He sort of got away. He's a chicken-shit, though, I figure he's long gone by now. If we got the videos, he's nothing to worry about."

Wright cursed loudly. "I'd say he's definitely something to worry about," he said. "Video or not, he knows what he saw. If he talks, we could end up in another mess."

"He's a coward, he isn't going to talk. Hell, he had that video all this time and never bothered to do anything with it except give it to that PI. He's probably on his way to Canada about now."

Forsyth shook his head, trying to keep up the act. "We better hope so. The last thing we need is for people to start asking questions about all this."

The four of them got back into their respective cars, and left the parking lot in different directions. Overhead, Mike had refocused the drone on to Driscoll's car, and the van pulled out a moment later.

Inside the van, Sam was staring wide-eyed at the receiver. "Marty's still alive? Lemmons sounded certain he was dead."

"Just means those two lied to him," Karen said. "Are you really surprised?"

Sam shook his head as the van rolled along the streets toward Lakewood. "Just that he isn't dead," he said. "I mean, I'm glad, maybe the guy can actually get back to his life one day soon. Right now, all I care about is staying close enough to these guys to make sure we can stop them before they do anything bad to Tracy."

* * * * *

Marty had made only one stop on his way into town, pulling into a truck stop to gas up. While he was pumping gas, though, he saw a sign advertising a special sale on police scanners in the store, and hurried inside to get one. He also picked up one of the cheap cell phones they sold, before getting back on the highway and driving on into Denver.

He found the frequency used by the Denver PD, but he didn't know the unit number for Driscoll and Slocum. He listened for a while, hoping to hear one of their voices and recognize it, but finally he had an idea.

He stopped the truck at a gas station and took out the cell phone and dialed the number for the police department. When the desk sergeant answered, he put on his best ethnic accent. "Yo, man, I'm trying to get hold of Officer Driscoll. Any chance you could tell him to meet me at the 7-Eleven at Colfax and King?"

"And who is this?" the sergeant asked.

"Man, this be Tyrone, I'm his snitch! I got some stuff he need to know!"

A minute later, he heard the dispatcher call out, "3-21, see a man called Tyrone at the 7-Eleven, Colfax and King."

Driscoll's voice came back on the radio. "3-21, 10-4."

Marty parked the truck on the curb on King Street, half a block away from the store. He only waited about ten minutes before the squad car pulled then, and he watched as Driscoll went inside, looking for whoever had called to meet him. He came out a few minutes later, looked around the lot and then got back into the car. When it pulled out onto Colfax, Marty took his foot off the brake and hurried to the stop sign.

Traffic was clear, so he pulled out and followed the squad car down the road. He didn't have a concrete plan, but he intended to put a stop to these two killers, no matter what it cost him.

The squad car followed Colfax for a while, but then made a sudden turn. Marty turned as well, but then hung back some distance. He didn't want them to realize they were being followed. He stayed on them as they took a convoluted route, cutting through residential areas, obviously on their way to somewhere important.

"Somewhere important" turned out to be a taco restaurant. Marty cruised past and pulled into another parking lot where he could keep an eye on the squad car, then was startled to see a second squad waiting in the back of the lot. Driscoll's car pulled up near it, and four officers climbed out of the two cars and stood facing each other.

Right there in front of him were all four of the uniform officers he'd seen on the video, he knew it. He tightened his grip on the revolver and told himself it was time to take them out, but he couldn't quite make himself put the truck back into gear. He reasoned that it would be smarter to wait until he could get them alone or in pairs, rather than trying to take on the foursome. He would only have the element of surprise for a second, and he didn't know if he could shoot them all before they could start shooting back.

Other than in video games, Marty had never actually fired a gun. His determination to become a killer started to waver on him. He sat and watched as the four talked, and when they finally got back into their cars and drove away, he continued to follow Driscoll and Slocum. Sooner or later they would stop, and Marty was determined to force himself to aim the gun and pull the trigger.

* * * * *

The van was following, as well, and it wasn't long before Jeff Donaldson realized that the pickup truck in

front of him was also tailing the squad car. He leaned
back in his seat and motioned for Ron to look ahead.

"See that truck? It's been right in front of us for the
last five minutes. Every time the cops make a turn, he
makes the same one."

"Interesting," Ron said. He turned around and
looked at Sam. "Any idea who else might be tailing
these guys? There's a Chevy 4x4 up ahead that's
staying right on them."

Sam climbed up toward the front of the van and
looked through the windshield. "No, not a clue," he
said. "Can you run the license plate?"

"I can," Mike said. "What is it?"

Sam read the plate number off, and Mike tapped it
into one of the three computers sitting on a shelf in
front of them. A moment later, he got a response.
"Belongs to someone named Albert Linden, lives out in
Colorado Springs."

Sam squinted his eyes and pursed his lips. "That
name sounds familiar, but I can't place it. Colorado
Springs? I don't think I know anybody there."

"Well, whoever it is, he seems to be just as
interested in our quarry as we are. Let's keep an eye on
him and see what happens."

"Agreed," Sam said. He turned and looked at Karen.
"This has got to be the weirdest case I've ever had."

"You won't get any argument out of me," she said.

"It's the first case I've ever seen that got me shot in the ass!"

Because of traffic and stoplights, the drive to Lakewood took nearly half an hour, and Sam began to wonder if Driscoll and Slocum had spotted the pickup truck that was tailing them. Whoever was driving it seemed to have some idea of what he was doing, though, because he was keeping a number of vehicles between them and switching from lane to lane whenever possible.

Suddenly, the squad car whipped into the parking lot of a convenience store, and Slocum got out of the passenger seat and went inside. Sam and the others watched on the screen displaying the drone's camera image as the pickup truck approached the lot as if it were going to go on past, but then turned in at the last moment. It screeched to a halt just behind the squad car, as Donaldson pulled the van over into another parking lot almost a block behind.

Sam leaned toward the screen. "What on earth is he doing?" he asked, but then a hand was extended from the driver's window and they saw two flashes of light. Sam blinked once, then yelled, "Oh, dear Lord, I think he just shot Driscoll!"

The truck shot forward and raced around the building, but they couldn't see where it went after that. The drone stayed in position as Officer Slocum came running out of the store with his pistol drawn. He pointed it in the direction the truck had gone, then turned and looked into the driver's seat of the car.

A moment later, he took a cell phone from his pocket and dialed the number frantically.

"Let's get up there," Sam said. "We've got to find out what's going on."

Ron looked at him. "Um, you and Ms. Karen are supposed to be dead, remember?"

"Well, what else can we do? If Driscoll's been shot, I may have just lost my last chance to get Tracy back safely."

"Then let's do this right," Karen said. "Somebody give me a phone."

Mike picked up a cell phone that was lying beside one of the computers and handed it to her. She quickly dialed the number, then spoke into the device. "This is Denver Homicide Detective Karen Parks," she said. "I need to speak with the District Attorney immediately."

Sam looked at her. "Are you sure this is a good idea?"

"It's better than charging into a potentially deadly situation. Hang on." She focused on the phone again. "Ma'am, this is Detective Karen Parks. I'm calling to notify you that I am currently conducting an investigation into criminal activities of ADA Monica Purvis and several Denver police officers, including orchestrating and concealing the murder of three teenagers. Those include Detective Jerry Lemmons, who was killed earlier today by one of the other officers." She listened for a moment, then looked into Sam's eyes. "Actually, ma'am, we have video and audio recordings to back up what I'm telling you, and one of the officers who was involuntarily involved has approached us and is willing to testify, but the situation has taken another turn. Mr. Prichard and I are currently following patrolmen Driscoll and Slocum, and it appears that one of them has just been shot." She listened for a moment, then nodded at Sam. "Ma'am, I would prefer if no one but you knows I'm coming. I had approached ADA Purvis with this earlier today, and she actually tried to have one of these officers kill me and Private Investigator Sam Prichard, who is working with me." She listened for another moment, then said, "Yes, ma'am," and then ended the call.

She looked at Sam. "She wants to see us as soon as possible, with the video and audio. I don't know her very well personally, but I get the feeling Monica is about to find herself in a whole world of trouble."

Sam rolled his eyes. "And just what am I supposed to do about Tracy? Those two are probably my last shot at finding her alive, I can't just forget about her." He punched the wall of the van, and then looked at Ron. "You got another copy of that video you can give her?"

"Yeah, it's on the computer."

"Then take her to the DA's office. I'm going to go find Tracy." He yanked open the side door of the van and stepped out, then began walking as quickly as his bad hip allowed toward the squad car two blocks ahead.

Karen called after him a couple of times, but Sam kept walking. A moment later, the little drone zipped by Sam's head and flew right into the van. A few seconds after that, the van started up and drove away.

18

Several people had gathered around the squad car by the time Sam arrived, and Slocum was leaning against the building as he spoke into a phone. Sam glanced into the car and saw that Driscoll was alive but bleeding at his left ear and shoulder. The injuries did not appear to be life threatening, so Sam stepped around the crowd and walked directly to Slocum.

The officer was speaking frantically into the phone, but Sam reached out and snatched the phone away, cutting off the call, and then grabbed Slocum by his shirt and slammed him against the wall.

"Where the hell is Tracy Jensen?" Sam asked, his voice cold and full of menace. Slocum stared into his face for a second, and then his eyes went wide in terror.

"Jesus," he cried out, "you're dead!"

"Not nearly as dead as you're about to be," Sam said, "if you don't show me where Tracy is right now."

Slocum shook his head as if to clear it. "You mean the woman Lemmons was holding? But I don't know, I don't know where she is. Hank knows, but I don't. That's where we were going, but somebody—oh my God, did you shoot him?"

Sam stared at the man in shock, then turned and looked back at Driscoll. Even as he did so, sirens were growing loud as police cars approached, and Sam knew he was running out of time. The sirens were growing a lot louder, and Sam wasn't sure what would happen when the new cops arrived. The word was still out that he had supposedly killed Lemmons, and cops don't like to arrest a cop killer. They figure the world is much better off if such a person never makes it to trial.

Sam let go of Slocum and backed away, then turned and hurried toward the back of the building. A man had just climbed out of a car and left it running, so Sam jumped in and threw it into reverse.

The car's owner began shouting at him, but Sam paid him no attention. He dropped the shifter into drive and floored the car, shooting out the back exit of the parking lot and turning onto a residential street. He drove three blocks, then made a left and was planning to make another right turn when he suddenly saw the Chevy truck sitting parked at the curb.

Instinct took over and Sam whipped the car in just ahead of the truck. He threw it into park and jumped out, drawing his own gun and aiming it at the windshield as he walked toward it, but then his eyes went wide. The driver of the truck was Marty Fletcher.

"Marty? What the hell are you doing?"

Marty looked up at him and Sam saw the tears streaming down his cheeks. "I had to stop them," he said. "They came out to your cabin and wanted to kill me, so I had to stop them."

Marty held up the revolver and Sam carefully reached out to take it from him. Marty surrendered it without a problem, and Sam laid it on the hood of the truck.

"Oh, geez, Marty," he said. "We were getting it all under control. It all would've been over in just a few minutes, and we were following them to where Tracy is. You can calm down, though, you didn't kill anyone. Driscoll is wounded but it's not serious."

Marty stared at him for a moment longer, and then hung his head in shame. He began to weep—great, wracking sobs that shook his entire body. "I'm sorry," he said, "I just couldn't take anymore. I couldn't keep hiding, I couldn't keep waiting for them to find me and kill me..."

Sam took a deep breath. Under the circumstances, and especially since it appeared Driscoll would survive, there was a good chance Marty would get off on self-defense, or at worst, a temporary insanity plea. He hooked a finger into the trigger guard of the revolver and picked it up again, then told Marty to slide over.

Sam got behind the wheel, shoving the revolver behind the seat of the truck, and then started it up and put it in gear.

Beauregard had said that Sam would have to solve the case all on his own. If that were true, then somehow Sam must be able to figure out where Tracy was being hidden. He drove Marty's stolen truck around the area slowly, trying to think of any way he might find her.

Marty was still whimpering on the passenger side, leaning against the window with his eyes closed. Sam glanced over at him and had a sudden thought. "Marty," he said, "that time Tracy brought Lemmons to see you, did he say anything about Lakewood?"

Marty shook his head, but didn't speak. Sam reached over and shook his shoulder gently. "Marty, think for a minute. We've got to find Tracy, and we need to do it soon. Did he say anything at all about having a place in Lakewood?"

Once again, Marty only shook his head. Sam slammed a hand on the steering wheel and then turned another corner.

"... *someplace in Lakewood...*" That was what Driscoll had said, that Lemmons had stashed Tracy in someplace in Lakewood. Sam racked his brain, trying to think of anyone who might have known Lemmons well enough to make an educated guess about what old house it might have been. There were lots of old houses in Lakewood, and it would probably take weeks to search them all.

Well, it would take weeks for humans to search them all. Sam reached into his pocket and took out his cell phone, then dialed the number Indie was using.

She answered before the first ring had finished. "Sam? Are you okay?"

"I'm fine, Babe," he said. "We are actually getting close to wrapping this up, I think, but I still haven't found Tracy. And incidentally, Marty isn't dead. In fact, he's right here with me at the moment."

"Oh, Sam, that's a relief. That'll at least get rid of that murder charge, right?"

"Yeah, it gets rid of that murder charge," he said, "but there's still the one where the local cops all think I killed Jerry Lemmons. Don't worry about that one, though, Karen Parks is getting that straightened out right now. The reason I called is because I got just a little information about Tracy. It turns out Lemmons was holding her in what's been referred to as 'someplace in Lakewood.' Can you get Herman to start digging and find out if there are any old houses in Lakewood that Lemmons might have been connected to? Maybe he owned one, or someone in his family did?"

"Yeah, I'll put him on it right now. Are you sure it's in Lakewood?"

"I'm not hundred percent sure of anything, but the one cop who knew something about it said that's where

Lemmons stashed her. Unfortunately, that was Officer Driscoll and Marty just shot him. I don't know how soon we're going to be able to talk to him, so I'm trying to figure out any other way possible to find her, and I'm kinda grasping at straws."

"Wait a minute, Marty shot one of these cops?"

"Yeah. I guess Driscoll was the one who went out to my cabin and tried to kill Marty. Somehow Marty got a gun and came out looking for him. Lucky for Driscoll, Marty isn't really all that good a shot."

Sam could tell she was confused, but all she said was, "Okay, I understand. Let me put Herman to pounding on this, and I'll call you back as soon as I get a result."

"Thanks, Babe," Sam said. "I love you, and tell Kenzie we should all be back home soon."

He ended the call and dialed a number Ron Thomas had given him. Ron answered on the fourth ring.

"Hello?"

"Ron, it's Sam. Is Karen still with you?"

"Yeah, just a minute." Sam heard a bit of shuffling, and then Karen came on the line. "I thought you'd like to know that Driscoll isn't dead, just got nicked on his ear and shoulder. In a strange twist of fate, the shooter was Marty Fletcher, and I've got him with me now. I'm driving the pickup truck he was in, which I assume is probably stolen, and doing everything I can to try to figure out where Tracy might be held."

"Well, why don't you just wait a little bit?" Karen asked. "I've been back and forth on the phone with the DA again, and she's issued warrants for Monica, Wright, Driscoll and Slocum. I'm sticking to our deal with Forsyth; as far as anyone knows, he volunteered to work with us when Monica told him to get rid of us. She went down the hall and arrested Monica personally, and already sent out the order to pick up the others. I'm having Forsyth brought to her office to corroborate my story."

"Good," Sam said. "Maybe Driscoll will give up Tracy in the hope of leniency. What do you want me to do now?"

"Why don't you bring Marty and come on over to the DA's office? Since he's the one who actually saw the video first, he's going to be an important witness."

"Uh-huh," Sam said. "Think there's any chance he might get immunity over shooting Driscoll? Any half-assed lawyer could probably get them off on self-defense anyway, don't you think?"

Karen chuckled. "Just bring him," she said. "I'll twist the DA's arm for that immunity, I think we can swing it."

Sam cut the call and looked over at Marty. "Well, this may all work out after all," he said. "Friend of mine, a homicide detective, thinks she can get you immunity on the shooting, because they're going to need you to testify against the cops who killed those kids."

Marty slowly turned his face to look at Sam. "You mean they're really going to go after them?"

Sam nodded his head. "They are," he said. "One thing you need to know, though, is that one of those cops has turned informant against them. It was Forsyth, the one who never touched those kids."

Marty's red-rimmed eyes looked at him for a moment, then he nodded. "He was the one who wanted to call for help, right?"

"Right. It's a long story, but it turns out there was an assistant district attorney involved in all this, and she actually told him to kill me and my friend in homicide. That's when he came to us and told us everything, so he's working with us now. You and I are going to go to the DA's office right now and help to get all this straightened out."

Sam made another turn and realized that he was about to go right past the convenience store where Marty had tried to kill Driscoll. He glanced into the parking lot as they drove slowly past and was delighted to see Slocum in handcuffs, bent over the back of the squad car. An ambulance was there, and he assumed that Driscoll was inside it. He focused on the road ahead, and made a slight detour into Arvada, where he locked up the Chevy truck and put Marty into Karen's Ford before going on to the DA. He retrieved Marty's tablet from under the seat as he drove.

Thirty minutes later, he was seated at a conference table in the DA's office, in the beginning of a meeting that lasted nearly three hours. Indie called him once, telling him that Herman had found no property in Lakewood that was connected to Jerry Lemmons. Sam relayed that information to everyone else in the room, which somehow even included Ron, Jeff and Mike. Three other ADAs were there helping to take notes, and Sam watched David Forsyth as he admitted to being terrified after what he'd seen. Sam and Karen both swore that Forsyth had voluntarily offered to help them after Monica Purvis told him to kill them, so the DA granted him full immunity on the murder charge.

Marty was also given immunity, since the DA said she could understand his fear. She did warn him, however, that taking the law into his own hands was always a mistake. He apologized several times, but hearing the whole story of how he had discovered the video and his terror of what might happen if it were discovered was enough to satisfy everyone there. Arrangements were even made to return the pickup truck he had "borrowed."

Slocum and Wright had been arrested and were currently sitting in the county jail. Driscoll had also been arrested, but he had been taken to St. Joseph's Hospital where he was undergoing surgery to reattach his left ear and remove a bullet from the joint of his left shoulder. The doctors said it would be at least another twenty-four hours before he could be questioned, and

Sam almost had to be restrained.

"Mr. Prichard," the DA said to him, "I understand your concern about Ms. Jensen, but there are certain protocols I have to follow when a suspect is wounded. We have to defer to the doctors on this, and there's nothing else I can do. I'm sure Ms. Jensen is probably uncomfortable, but I doubt another day will cost her her life."

Sam stared at her. "Is there anything else you need from me at this moment?"

"Just your signature on your statement," the DA said. Sam scribbled his name and then stormed out of the conference room.

By the time Sam stepped out the front door of the building, it was a little after eight PM and the sun was getting low in the sky. The DA had announced that Sam would not be facing any murder charges, and the word had spread quickly through the police department. A couple of officers standing in front of the building congratulated him and shook his hand as he walked toward the parking lot.

He climbed into Karen's old pickup truck and started it up, then took out his phone and called Indie.

"Sam? How's it going?"

"Well, I've been cleared on the murder charges," he said. "Driscoll had surgery, and the doctors say we won't be able to question him about Tracy until sometime tomorrow afternoon. How far away are you?

I think it's safe to come home now."

Indie giggled. "We're at the Holiday Inn in Boulder. Your mom charged the room to her office credit card, so we wouldn't be that easy to find. I doubt they'd think of checking your mom's boss's card, right? I'll get us checked out and we can be home in a couple of hours."

"Good," Sam said with a smile. "I've missed you."

"Ditto," Indie said.

"It's just frustrating about Tracy. I wish I had my phone, I could at least call Heather and let her know there's a good chance we're going to find her mom tomorrow."

"I've got her number," Indie said. "I grabbed our notes before I left the house last night. Want me to give it to you?"

Sam grinned and shook his head. "Baby, I should've known you'd have it. Yeah, what is it?"

Indie told him the number, and Sam ended the call and dialed it immediately. The teenager answered the phone cautiously. "Hello?"

"Heather? This is Sam Prichard."

"Oh, yes, Mr. Prichard! Mr. Prichard, did you find my mom?"

Sam grimaced. "Well, not yet," he said. "We did get to the bottom of the trouble she and Marty were in, but it turns out there was a police detective involved and he apparently locked her up somewhere. We've got one guy who knows where she is, but he got hurt today and had to have surgery. We won't get to talk to him until tomorrow, but I'm sure your mom will be all right until then."

Sam could tell the girl was crying when she spoke again. "Oh, please find her," she said. "My stepdad just sits and stares at the wall, he doesn't know what to do without her, and neither do I."

"I can understand that," Sam said. "I don't know what I'd do if my wife was missing like this, but I promise you I'll do everything I can to bring her home by tomorrow. Just hang in there, okay?"

The girl promised her that she would try, and said goodbye to Sam. He put the phone back in his pocket with a heavy heart.

Sam headed for home. In the morning, he would see about getting the corvette out of impound, but it had been an awfully long day and he was ready to relax with his family.

19

Indie, Kenzie and the grandmothers all rolled in just before eleven, and found Sam asleep on the couch. Kenzie decided there was simply no sense in that, so she ran over and threw herself on him, giving him a hug that woke him with a smile. He sat up and held her tight for a moment, then wrapped one arm around his wife.

Indie let Kenzie wind down for a few minutes, letting the excitement of seeing her daddy help the child burn up her last burst of energy for the day, and then walked her up the stairs to her bedroom. She was back down only a few moments later, and announced that Kenzie had gone right to sleep.

The four adults sat and talked for a little bit, while Sam brought them all up to date on his adventures. It was obvious that he was frustrated, and finally it boiled over.

"Kim," Sam said, "I want you to tell Beauregard

that the next time he sticks his nose into one of my cases, he'd better have more information. I don't know which three lives he felt I needed to save, but Marty is okay, and I hope to bring Tracy home tomorrow sometime. Assuming they were two of them, I sure would like to know who was the third."

His mother-in-law looked at him sheepishly. "I know, Sam," she said. "Sometimes he just drives me crazy. Like tonight, we were on the way here and all of a sudden he pops up and says, 'Tell Sam he isn't done.' I mean, what is that supposed to mean?"

Sam stared at her for a long moment. "Can you talk to him whenever you want?" Sam asked.

She shook her head. "Not really," she said. "Well, I can talk to him, but that doesn't mean he's going to answer me. He only talks when he wants to."

Sam's mother, Grace, turned around and looked at her. "Kim, now you know that's not true. You know how to make him talk."

"Whoa, whoa," Sam said. "Mom, what are you talking about?"

"She's full of it," Grace said. "She can go into that weird trance of hers whenever she wants, she just hates to do it."

Sam turned back to his mother-in-law. "Kim? Is there a way you can ask him point-blank questions?"

Kim was giving Grace what could only be called a nasty look. "Well, there's a way, but it's really—it's just really uncomfortable."

Sam sat there in silence for a moment and counted to ten in his head. "But you love me, right? So, you help me out with this, right?"

Kim frowned at Grace, then turned to face Sam with a sigh. "I guess I can try," she said. "No promises, though, he can be pretty cantankerous when he wants to be." She settled back into her chair and got comfortable, then turned to Sam again. "What do you want to know?"

Sam's eyebrows shot up. "The same thing I wanted to know all along," he said, "I want to know where Tracy is."

Kim rolled her eyes, then leaned her head back and closed them. Just a moment later, her face seemed to go slack. They all watched her as her breathing deepened, and a minute passed in silence. She took a deep breath all of a sudden, and her eyes popped open. They rolled around for a moment, and then focused on Sam.

"Samuel," she said in the deep, southern drawl that meant Beauregard had taken control. "Your work is not yet finished, son. You have saved two of the three lives, in Mr. Fletcher and Officer Forsyth, but you must still save the woman. You are not done."

Sam felt the eerie chill down his spine that always came whenever he was face to face with Kim's subconscious alter ego. "What is that supposed to mean? And don't give me any of your vague hints, I want you to spell it out, this time."

There was something about the look in Kim's eyes that made Sam feel as if he were being scolded, and then that voice continued. "The woman is still in grave danger," it said. "You cannot wait until tomorrow, you must find her before sunrise."

Sam gave an exasperated gasp. "And just how the hell do you propose I do that? Can't you just tell me where she is?"

"Samuel, it does not work that way. Where I exist, there are only thoughts, and sometimes they reach me. I know that she is in danger, but I do not know what kind of danger it is. I do not know where she is, only that you must find her before it is too late. I do not know how you will find her, but I know that you already possess the knowledge that can lead you to her."

Sam shook his head. "I already possess...What are you talking about? I don't have the slightest idea where to look for her, except that it's supposed to be in Lakewood."

"Then I suppose you must consider what you know about Lakewood and this man who took the woman. Somehow, you already know what you need to know; now all you must do is find out what it is that you know."

Sam rolled his eyes, exasperated. "Well, hell," he said. "What did you mean about me having to find her before sunrise? Can you at least tell me that?"

Kim tilted her head to one side, and her eyes bored into Sam's own. "If you do not find her before the sun rises over this city, she will not be survive. I do not know exactly what will happen, but something at that time will cause her death."

Kim shook suddenly, and a second later her eyes opened. She looked around as if confused, then focused on Sam.

"Did he come?" she asked.

"Yeah," Sam growled, "but he left me just as much in the dark as I already was."

"Sam," Indie said, "think! What could you possibly know about any connection between Lemmons and Lakewood?"

"I don't know!" Sam said, exasperated. "He never mentioned anything about Lakewood at all, and the only one who knows anything is Driscoll, and he's in the freaking hospital under anesthesia!" He sat for a moment, and then got to his feet. "I'm going down to talk to him," he said.

"Sam, they'll never let you get near him, not this late at night."

Sam grinned at his wife. "Who said I was going to ask permission?"

He stalked out the door and got into the truck, then headed for St. Joseph's Hospital. It took him nearly twenty minutes to get there even with the light nighttime traffic, and he had to go in through the emergency room entrance.

Driscoll had been in surgery a few hours before, but he should have been out of recovery by the time Sam got there. That meant he'd be in a regular room, but since he was a suspect in multiple murders, Sam knew he'd have no trouble finding the right room. He'd just look for the one with a cop on guard outside.

He found it ten minutes later, on the third floor. A uniform officer was sitting in a chair beside the door, and he looked up with a smile as he recognized Sam.

"Hey, Sam," he said. "A little late to be coming to visit anyone. What's up?"

The cop was one Sam knew pretty well, a guy named Larry Wyant. Larry had been a close friend of Sam's old partner, Dan Jacobs, and Dan had brought him to Sam's house during a few of the barbecues he'd thrown after his retirement.

"Hi, Larry," he said. "Yeah, it's late, but I need to talk to your guy in there. He's the only one who knows where a woman is being held, and I need to find her as soon as possible."

Larry frowned. "Sam, I'm not supposed to let anyone in."

"Yeah, I know," Sam said, "but this is kind of urgent. I've been told that if I don't find her before morning, it may well be too late, and I promised this lady's little girl I'd bring her home safe. All I need is a few minutes, I just need him to tell me where she is, and then I'm gone. I promise."

Larry chewed his cheek for a second, but then he grinned. "Okay, but just a few minutes. Come on." He turned and opened the door into the room, and then he suddenly froze. "Oh, crap," he said, and Sam leaned around to look past him.

Driscoll was lying on the bed in the room, but something was obviously wrong. His eyes were wide open, and his face had a bluish cast, but what caught Sam's eye instantly was the fact that the entire bed and part of the floor were covered in blood.

Larry and Sam entered the room cautiously, but it was clear that Driscoll was dead. Somehow, he had managed to break a glass quietly enough that no one had heard it, and used the sharp edge to cut his own throat. Since he was not considered to be in any danger after his surgery, he hadn't been connected to a monitor, so no alarms had gone off to alert anyone.

"Jesus," Larry said. "I just checked on him like half an hour ago, and he was sleeping just fine!"

Sam pointed at the broken glass. "Looks like he woke up and realized what was going on, and decided he didn't want to face what was coming. He killed himself to get out of going to prison." Sam looked at the cop. "You better notify the nurse's station."

Larry nodded. "Yeah," he said. "And you better go on. I don't really want to explain that I was breaking rules and letting you in to talk to my prisoner."

Sam took one last look at Driscoll, then turned away without another word. He made it to the elevator without being seen and hurried back out to the truck.

He looked at the clock on the stereo and sighed. Sunrise was less than six hours away and he had no idea how to find Tracy. As much as he refused to believe that Beauregard was really an old civil war ghost, he couldn't deny that he'd been right on many occasions; Sam felt a sinking in his heart as he thought about Tracy, about her daughter and how he was going to live with himself if he failed to find her in time.

Think, he told himself. *Beauregard says I already know what I need to know, so what do I know about sunrise? What could possibly happen at 6:08 AM that would mean Tracy wouldn't survive?*

There were very few things Sam could imagine that would work on such a timetable and could cause someone to die, but he tried listing them off. Could it be that she was chained to a bomb that would go off then? That sounded like something out of an old movie, not like something Jerry Lemmons might actually have done. That would make as much sense as tying her to a railroad track and waiting for a train to come along, and Sam just couldn't imagine something like that happening in real life.

Timetables, timetables…What else operated on a timetable that was set ahead of time? He thought about everything he could possibly identify as being set on a timetable as he drove around the city, but nothing he imagined seemed to be applicable to the situation.

Okay, he thought, *let's forget about the timetables themselves, what about the way they're set up?* Trains and buses run on timetables, but those are set by operators who calculate the time it takes to get from one point to another. TV and radio programs run on timetables, but they're set by program managers. What else, what else?

A light ahead of him turned red and Sam came to a stop. He continued thinking while he waited for it to turn green, and the thought crossed his mind that traffic lights fit the bill. Their scheduling was flexible and changed throughout the day, depending on traffic patterns and such, but those were handled by computers. Was there something controlled by a computer that could possibly relate to this situation?

The more he thought about it, the more frustrated he got. What on earth could possibly happen precisely at sunrise that could result in Tracy's death?

Sam glanced at the clock again and saw that it was almost two in the morning. Slightly over four hours to go, and he was no closer to figuring it out than he had been two mornings before, when Heather had come to him. Sam could barely recall the feelings he had once had for Tracy, but that didn't change the fact that she deserved to live, that her daughter deserved to have her back. Sam's stomach was tying itself in knots as he tried desperately to figure out his next move.

20

The ringing of his phone startled him. Sam snatched it out of his pocket expecting to see Indie's number on the display, but it wasn't. The number looked familiar, though, so Sam answered.

"Hello?"

A soft voice spoke. "Mr. Prichard, I'm sorry to bother you so late..."

Sam recognized Heather's voice. "It's no bother, Heather," he said. "Just want you to know, I'm still out looking for your mom."

"I just—I couldn't sleep, so I was listening to the radio in my room and I heard the news. They're talking about my mom, about how that detective hid her somewhere and nobody knows where."

"Yeah, that's true. Don't give up on me yet, though. I won't stop 'til I bring her home to you."

"I never did like that guy," Heather said. "He was always going on and on about how he was going to get rich someday, but I think he didn't like it when I was around."

Sam's eyebrows lowered, as he tried to figure out what she was saying. "What guy is that, Heather?"

"That Mr. Lemmons, that detective. He dated my mom for a little while, but that was before she met Gary. I think he always just wanted Mom to himself, because he was always trying to take her places where kids couldn't go. It just makes me sick to know that he's the one who did this to her."

Sam started to nod and express his sympathy, but then another thought occurred to him. "Heather," he said, "did he ever talk about anything in Lakewood?"

"Lakewood? Not that I can remember. Why?"

"I just wondered," Sam said. "Earlier today, one of the people involved with him said something about how he might have hidden your mom in Lakewood, but I don't know where."

"No, I don't remember anything about Lakewood. He never really talked about places, just about how he was making a lot of money with his side business."

A tingle started at the back of Sam's neck, and he felt those little hairs began to rise. "What kind of side business was he in, Heather? Do you know?"

The girl laughed softly, but there was a sadness in it. "Oh, yeah," she said. "That was pretty much all he talked about whenever I was around. I guess he used to blow stuff up when he was in the Navy or something, and he says he's really good at it. He started a business where he works for different companies that want to tear down buildings. He could set it up so they kinda fell down, just by the way he put his bombs inside. He even took us to watch a couple times while he blew up a building. I guess it was kind of interesting, if you like that kind of stuff."

"There's an old empty apartment building at Wadsworth and Florida..." *"Traffic will be rescheduled during the demolition of this building..."* *"Making Way For Progress."*

South Wadsworth Boulevard met West Florida Avenue in Lakewood!

"Heather," Sam said, "I think you may have just given me an idea. I don't want to get your hopes up too high just yet, but I think I might know where your mom is. I'll call you back in just a little bit and let you know if I was right, okay?"

The girl's voice suddenly had hope in it. "Really? Okay, I'll be right here."

Sam checked the signs at the next intersection and realized he was almost into Littleton, so he whipped the wheel to the right and fishtailed around the corner. The big 460 roared as he shoved his foot to the floor, but three miles later he had to brake again so that he could make the next turn. That put him on Wadsworth, going north. He kept his foot down on the accelerator, flashing his lights constantly to make the traffic signals think he was an ambulance. Each light turned green as he approached, and Sam flew around the few vehicles that were on the street.

There! The next intersection was Florida Avenue, and there was the abandoned apartment building. Sam heard the brakes squeal as he slid the truck into the parking lot. As soon as he was stopped, he slammed it into park and was out and running toward the boarded-up front doors.

The streetlights on the corner were bright enough to illuminate the warning signs that were screwed to the building. They warned that the building was scheduled for implosion at 6:15 in the morning, and repeated the information that traffic would be diverted away from the intersection for a few hours.

The plywood over the doors was secured with heavy screws, and Sam couldn't get a grip on them. He ran limping back to the truck and started digging through it, shouting with excitement when he came up with a tire iron. Taking it back to the door, he managed to jam the pointed end in behind one edge of the plywood, and then began the painstaking task of prying it a little at a time away from the structure.

It was slow going, but after fifteen minutes he managed to get one side lose. He dropped the tire iron and grabbed it with both hands, wrenching backward and finally snapping it free. The original doors had been removed, and he was looking into a dark hallway.

Sam reached into his pocket and produced the small LED flashlight he always carried. He flicked it on and shined it into the dark, gaping maw ahead of him, then slowly began following the hallway.

"Tracy?" Sam shouted. "Tracy, it's Sam Prichard! If you can hear me, make some noise, I'm trying to find you."

There was no response. Sam moved through the first floor, shining the light into each apartment he came to, and hurriedly searching through several of them. The building had been stripped of fixtures like doors, windows, lights and plumbing, leaving mostly just bare walls. That made it easy to look into every room, but the building was four stories high and almost a block long. At a rough guess, Sam figured there could be as many as eighty apartments inside.

Sam followed every hall, made every turn and checked every apartment he came to. When he had finished the first floor, he climbed up the stairs to the second and repeated his search pattern, calling out for Tracy the whole time. After nearly 40 minutes, he had finished searching the first two floors and moved to the third.

As he moved from apartment to apartment, Sam had to fight down the doubts that began to assail him. Realistically, he knew, there was no way to be sure that this was one of the buildings Jerry would demolish, but it fit completely with everything Beauregard had said. Jerry had suggested it as a meeting place, which implied he had some connection to it, so Sam already possessed knowledge of this building, and it would certainly be a dangerous place to be around sunrise. If Tracy was not out by then, she would almost certainly die and her body might not even be found in the rubble.

He found nothing on the third floor, and forced himself to climb up to the fourth. He'd been in the building for more than an hour, calling out to Tracy the whole time with no response. By the time he finished clearing the fourth floor, he was beginning to feel like there was no hope of finding her in time.

When he returned to the stairway, Sam leaned on it for a few moments and tried to fight off the despair that wanted to settle in. It was probably close to four by then, which meant he had barely more than two hours to go. He made his way slowly down the stairs and toward the door he had ripped open.

He walked outside and circled the building, looking for anything big enough to hold a person. Considering everything Lemmons had done, Sam wouldn't put it past him to have locked Tracy into a barrel beside the building, but there was nothing. He made a complete circuit but didn't find anything that might conceal anything bigger than a small child.

He started back toward the pickup, trying to think of

where else he might look, when a piece of plywood that seemed out of place caught his eye. Both the front and rear doors of the building were raised a few feet above the ground, and there were steps and a small porch at each one. This piece of plywood looked like it might be covering a door, but it was flush with the concrete walkway that circled the building. Sam stared at it for a moment, then walked as quickly as he could back to the front door. He retrieved the tire iron he had dropped there and hurried back again.

This particular sheet of plywood was secured even better than the other one, and it took Sam another half-hour to rip it free. Sure enough, there was a low open doorway behind it, but this one opened on stairs leading down.

It was a maintenance cellar, a partial basement that allowed plumbers and electricians to access the pipes and wiring and such that made it possible for so many people to live in a single building. Sam shined his light down the stairs and moved down them as quickly as he could.

When he reached the bottom, he saw that most of the plumbing and wiring had already been removed. There were stanchions all around, supports to help hold up the floors above, but little else, and each stanchion had a small barrel strapped to its base, and each barrel had a timer sitting on top of it.

Those barrels, Sam knew, would be the explosives

that would bring the building down when they were detonated. Each of the timers was counting down, and they all indicated there was less than ninety minutes to go.

Sam thought about trying to disarm or disengage the timers, but that wasn't something he actually knew how to do. He forced himself to ignore the explosives and began searching the room. It was just big enough that the light couldn't quite reach from one side to the other, so he walked through it, shining it everywhere he could.

"Tracy?" he shouted again. "Tracy, it's Sam, yell out if you're here!"

She had to be there somewhere, he kept telling himself. This was the only possible place that fit everything. It was in Lakewood, as Driscoll had said, it was scheduled for demolition at dawn as Beauregard had hinted, and it was the only thing connected to the entire case that might fit Beauregard's insistence that Sam already knew something about the place where Tracy could be found. She simply had to be there.

The maintenance cellar was under one whole half of the building, but there was a solid concrete wall at the point where he thought the center of the building should be. He put his ear against it and listened, but heard nothing.

Sam turned and shined the light around, and it appeared to him that all of the pipes and conduit of the building might have come into this one section. If that were the case, then Tracy was nowhere to be found in the structure.

On the other hand, it was possible there was a separate basement for the other side of the building. He didn't remember seeing another access door, but with just over an hour to go before sunrise, he felt he had to be certain. He made his way back to the stairs and out into the parking lot, then began walking around the building once more. He kept the light shining on the wall as he walked, and this time he carried the tire iron with him.

There it was! On the back of the building, there was another sheet of plywood screwed to the wall, just over the walkway. Sam attacked it like a madman, but this one was just as solid as the other. He tried to pry it off for a couple of minutes, then grabbed his phone to call for help.

Still no signal! he thought in frustration, but then the reason for it became obvious. The explosives that were all in place were probably controlled by a computer that would send a signal at the pre-set time, so there was something set up around the building that would cancel out any other kind of signal. He'd read an article about that once, how cell phones could be blocked in situations like that.

Sam looked down the street and thought about trying to go far enough to get out of the damping field, but with his hip screaming and the truck away on the far side of the building, he couldn't risk the time. If Tracy was in there, she didn't have a lot of time to spare, so he decided to keep at it alone and hope the demolition crew would show up early enough to help, or stop the explosions. He worked at the door for almost half an hour before he finally got one side loose enough to hook his fingers into it.

This sheet was also thicker than the other one. Sam couldn't tear it completely free, so finally, he pried it out as far as he could and slipped between it and the doorjamb.

The light illuminated the stairs, and he held onto the handrails as he made his way down. He started yelling for Tracy before he ever got to the bottom, and stopped to listen for any response.

Nothing. Still, he wasn't going to leave without checking, so he began walking around the big empty space. Like the other one, the stanchions had barrels of explosives strapped to their bases, and he could see the timers counting down until the explosion—less than forty minutes to go. All of the pipes and wiring had already been removed, but there were pieces of conduit hanging from the ceiling, and he had to dodge around them. There was also ductwork, probably from the old air conditioning and heating system. It struck him as odd that those things had been removed from the other side and left in this one, but he supposed it was possible the workers had simply run out of time. He kept calling

Tracy's name as he made his way through the cellar, but she didn't respond.

His heart sinking, he finally turned around to start back for the stairs. This site had been such an obstacle course that it had taken quite a while to go through it, and he figured he had less than half an hour to go before the police and demolition crew would arrive to block the streets and supervise the blast. He swung the light around as he walked, silently praying for an answer.

21

There was a metal box over against one wall, and Sam had initially dismissed it as part of the ductwork, but when the light shone on it again he thought it seemed out of place. He turned away from the stairs to inspect it more closely, and he noticed a foul odor as he got closer.

It was hollow, and not very heavy. Sam shoved it sideways and it slid away with little resistance, and suddenly the odor was worse. He gagged once and covered his face with his arm, and that's when he saw that there was a square hole in the concrete wall. He squatted down and pointed the light inside, and a pair of frightened eyes looked back at him.

Tracy was sitting at the back of a cavity that had been dug into the dirt, her arms and legs secured with zip ties to the wooden framework that kept it from collapsing. A cloth was wrapped around her face, and

Sam was sure that she was gagged as well.

He turned the light to the side, and then he gagged again. Only a few feet away from Tracy, Sam could see what he was certain were the decomposing bodies of the teenagers he'd seen murdered in the video. He turned the light away from them and focused it back on Tracy's face, and that's when he saw the tears running down her cheeks.

"Been looking for you," Sam said. He stuffed the flashlight into his mouth, reached into his pocket for the Swiss Army knife he always carried and began crawling into the putrid space. Cutting the zip ties loose took only a few seconds, but when Tracy reached for the gag, he told her she should wait. She glanced in the direction of the bodies and then looked back at him and nodded.

Her arms and legs were weak, and Sam ended up half dragging her out of the cavity. Once they got into the maintenance cellar, he reached up and took the gag away, and she started working her jaw. Sam glanced at the nearest timer and saw that it was down to only twenty-two minutes until detonation.

"Think you can stand?" Sam asked, and she nodded her head. Sam got to his feet and extended a hand, but he had to help support her once she was up. He led her to the stairs and helped her get up them, then walked her around the building to the pickup truck, dropped its tailgate and helped her to sit down.

"Hey!" Sam looked toward the sound of the voice and saw a man wearing a hard hat standing outside the fence. "What are you doing in there? That building is about to blow up, get out of there!" There was a squad car sitting in the intersection, and Sam figured there were others not far away.

Sam hobbled quickly over to the fence and looked the man in the eye. "Is there any way to stop the explosion? My name is Sam Prichard, I'm a private investigator, and I've just found the bodies of three murder victims in there."

The man's eyes looked like they were going to explode, and he grabbed a walkie-talkie out of his pocket. "George? George, we have to abort! Kill the countdown and get in there and disconnect everything, and send one of those cops over here to me right now!"

Suddenly there was a flurry of activity, as a couple of men ran into the sub basements of the building, and two police officers hurried over to where Sam was standing with the demolition man. Sam explained quickly what was going on, and one of the officers started issuing orders.

Within ten minutes, six more squad cars converged on the place, and a few minutes later there arrived a pickup truck bearing the markings of the Medical Examiner.

Another man from the demolition company came over to them as well, holding what looked like a laptop and tapping on the keyboard.

"I deactivated the timers, it's okay," he said. "Our guys have gone in and completely disconnected everything, so it's all safe now."

Sam leaned against the fence and breathed a sigh of relief. "Any chance you can shut down whatever it is that keeps cell phones from working? I need to make a couple of calls in a hurry."

"Already did," said the man with the computer. "That was one of the first things the cops asked for."

Sam thanked him, and hobbled a little more slowly back to where Tracy was sitting on the tailgate. He took out his phone and tapped Heather's number, then just handed it over. Tracy held it to her ear, and tears suddenly began streaming down her face when she heard her daughter's voice.

The construction company officials were informed that their building was considered a crime scene, and they didn't argue. One of them even thanked Sam for getting Tracy out and calling police. Had she died in the explosion, they would have been exposed to lawsuits that could have cost them millions.

Tracy reached out and tapped Sam on the shoulder, then handed him his phone. "Thank you," she croaked. He knew it was going to be a while before her voice would sound normal, but the police had said there was an ambulance on the way to take her to the hospital to be checked out. Heather and her stepfather would meet up with her there.

Sam looked at the phone in his hand and called Indie. He wasn't surprised when she answered on the second ring, but he could hear the residue of sleep in her voice.

"Sam? Are you okay?"

"I'm fine, Babe," he said. "Tell your mom's spooky old friend that we did it. I found Tracy, and I also found the bodies of those poor kids."

Indie hesitated for a moment. "And Tracy—is she okay?"

"She's stiff and sore, and she's been trapped in what amounted to a grave for several days. She will survive, but I'm sure it's been pretty rough on her."

"You sound pretty worried about her," Indie said. "Anything I should be concerned about?"

Sam's eyebrows shot up and tried to climb over his forehead. "About Tracy? Baby, that was over long before I ever met you," he said.

"Yeah, but sometimes an old flame can flare up when you least expect it."

Sam shook his head, but he was grinning. "Indie, I'll let you in on a secret. If things had ever worked out between me and Tracy, I probably would've been reasonably happy, but it was destined to come to an end anyway."

"Oh? What makes you say that?"

Sam smiled into the phone. "Because sooner or later I would have run into you," he said. "I'm absolutely certain that God wanted us together, babe, so He would've made sure I was available when that happened."

"Awww," Indie said, "that's so sweet. I love you."

"I love you too," Sam said, "and we'll discuss that in more detail when I get home in a little while."

"Is that a promise?"

"Absolutely," Sam said. "Just let me finish up here, and I'll be on the way."

Sam put the phone back in his pocket as the paramedics arrived and loaded Tracy into the back of their ambulance, then went in search of whoever was going to be handling the crime scene. One of the police officers pointed him toward a man in a suit, but another car came roaring in before Sam got to him. Karen Parks jumped out, her hair looking un-brushed and with no makeup on, which told Sam she'd been sleeping soundly when she got the call.

"Sam Prichard," she yelled as she stomped toward him, "what in the world have you done now?"

"Not a lot," Sam said. "Found the missing woman, located the missing bodies of our teenage murder victims, saved the day—you know, the usual." He couldn't help grinning at her, and the scowl on her face slowly faded as a grin of her own appeared.

"They called me out because of joint jurisdiction,"

she said. "Since the original murders and abduction happened in Denver, but the bodies and victim were found here, I've got to work with Lakewood detectives on this. We're going to need statements from you, but we can do that later. I gather you been up all night?"

Sam nodded. "Yes, and it's been a long one. You know how to reach me, so I'm going home and going to bed."

Karen shook her head, still grinning. "Go for it," she said. "I promise not to call until at least after lunchtime."

Sam nodded, climbed into the pickup truck and drove away.

22

Two days had passed since he had dragged Tracy out of that pit, but Sam didn't think he was ever going to get the smell of decomposition out of his sinuses. That thought rolled sleepily through his mind as he lay in bed, once again trying to catch the opportunity to sleep in.

There was, he thought, some sort of conspiracy that was designed to make sure he didn't get the chance. That conspiracy was evidenced on this particular morning by the ringing of the house phone. He started to roll out of bed to go and answer it, but the thunder of tiny, running feet rolled down the stairs and Kenzie beat him to it. Sam slid his feet into his slippers and listened as she answered the phone.

"Hello," she said. "Yeah, but he's asleep. Who? Just a minute, I'll go see if he'll wake up." The receiver thumped as she dropped it onto the table, and Sam

229

caught her up into a hug as he stepped out of his bedroom.

"Daddy! There's a man on the phone who wants to talk to you, his name is—I can't remember."

Sam chuckled and kissed her on the cheek. "Okay," he said, "I'll see who it is." He picked up the receiver and held it to his ear. "Sam Prichard."

"Sam? It's Travis Bittner."

Sam's eyebrows shot up. Travis Bittner was a Grammy-winning country singer, and Sam and his band had recently opened for one of his concerts in Denver. It'd been a wonderful experience, and Bittner had even sung a duet with Sam on one of the songs he had written.

"Yes, sir," Sam said. "What can I do for you?"

"Well, there's actually a couple of things I want to talk to you about," Bittner said. "First, I want to record a couple of your songs, so I was wondering if you're available to come to Nashville for a couple of weeks."

"Seriously? Man, that would be fantastic. When would I have to come?"

"We'll be in the studio all the rest of this month, and I'd like to work on your songs next week if possible. Could you make it by then?"

Sam felt a hand on his back and turned to see Indie looking up at him, curious. He winked at her and said, "Sure, that's no problem. We could use a bit of a vacation, anyway."

Bittner chuckled. "Well, it'll be a working vacation, but I think I can show you and the family a good time while you're here. But that brings up the other thing I need to talk to you about, so you might want to sit down."

"Sit down? Well, okay..." Sam sat down on a chair beside the kitchen table, and Indie sat beside him. Little Kenzie, who was watching both of her parents, climbed into her mother's lap. "Okay, I'm sitting. What's up?"

Bittner took a deep breath. "Sam, I want to steal your band."

Sam blinked. "Steal my band? What, all of them?"

"Yeah, if I can get away with it. Listen, Sam, you are a very good singer, and I mean that from the bottom of my heart. If I'm going to be truthful, however, you're not quite an incredible singer, and that's what it takes to really make it in country music today. I'm not trying to hurt your feelings or insult you, I'm just trying to be completely honest."

"You're not hurting my feelings," Sam said. "To be completely honest, you're not telling me anything I don't already know. But what's this got to do with the band?"

"It's got to do with the fact that I have stumbled across an incredible singer, a young woman with a unique voice and more talent in her pinky than I got in my whole body. The only thing she needs is an incredible band, and I believe she can make it to the top. I've given this a lot of thought, Sam, and I think your band is exactly what she needs to have a shot at making it all the way."

Sam shook his head in surprise. "They're definitely good," he said. "Have you talked to Chris or any of them about this yet?"

"Of course not, Sam," Bittner said. "They're your band, I wouldn't go to them behind your back. If you're not willing to let them go, they'll never even know I asked."

Indie was sitting close enough to be able to hear both sides of the conversation, and her eyes were locked onto Sam's own. He winked at her, and she broke into a smile. "Travis, I like being a country singer," he said, "but I know I'm not any kind of superstar. The band, on the other hand, those guys are great. Chris has had a shot at stardom before that he missed out on, partly because he didn't want to leave the others. If you are telling me you want the whole band, then I'm all for it. They deserve this kind of break."

Bittner laughed. "Sam, I was pretty sure that's how you feel," he said, "and that's why I'm calling you from the Denver airport. I flew in this morning on a ridiculously early flight. Think maybe you could get the band together today, so we can all sit down and discuss it?"

"I'd be delighted. How about I come on out to the airport and pick you up now, and you can hang out with me in the family until they all drag their lazy butts out of bed? I don't think any of them gets up before eleven, but we can probably get them all over here for lunch and spring it on them then."

"That sounds like a plan," Bittner said. "Don't come get me, though, I can take a taxi to your place. Want me to pick anything up on the way?"

Indie pantomimed cooking, so Sam grinned. "Nope. But bring your appetite, Indie is in the mood to cook a big breakfast."

"Oh, now that sounds good. I'll be there in thirty minutes!"

Indie hurried back to the bedroom and got dressed, then went to the kitchen and set the oven for biscuits while Sam shaved and dressed. By the time Bittner arrived, he was treated to biscuits with sausage gravy, scrambled eggs and bacon, and he shortly proclaimed it the best breakfast he'd had in years.

Bittner had brought a guitar, and it wasn't long before he and Sam were jamming in the living room. "Hey, Sam," Bittner said, "I've got this song I've been working on, but I'm stuck. Maybe you can help me finish it off."

He played and sang a verse, then the two of them talked about where the song was going, and Sam suggested a new approach on the chorus.

"Sam, I think that might be exactly what it needs. Sing it once, let's see how it goes."

Sam strummed his guitar for a moment, finding the melody, then began to sing.

" Wasn' that long ago that we made love,

Lying 'neath an open sky with just the stars above,

A blanket for a pillow and a sad song playing on the radio,

Wasn' that long ago that we said I do,

I couldn't believe that my own dreams were coming true,

Now you say you're leavin' and you need a little time,

Is there nothing I can say to keep you by my side?

But wait! I know you heard that sound,

Like a southbound freight train, it shakes the ground,

Did you hear the earthquake, and tell me,

How could you tell with all the noise you were makin'?

Did it open up your ears and spin your head around?

Did you ever wonder how the sound of silence can feel like thunder?

Tell me, are you hurtin' now?

Come on, baby, tell me what you're thinking,
Now that you've heard the sound
Of my heart breaking

I asked God for an angel with broken wings,
So I could take care of her and mend a few things,
Now that you're strong enough I guess that I can let you fly,
Just listen closely one more time 'fore you say goodbye,
Did you hear the earthquake, and tell me,
How could you tell with all the noise you were makin'?
Did it open up your ears and spin your head around?
Did you ever wonder how the sound of silence can feel like thunder?
Tell me, are you hurtin' now?
Come on, baby, tell me what you're thinking,
Now that you've heard the sound
Of my heart breaking
Of my heart breaking"

Indie and Kenzie both burst into applause, and Bittner's smile couldn't have been wider. "You did it, Sam," he said. "That twist was exactly what it needed."

He turned and looked at Indie. "You're not going to get mad if I show up on your doorstep now and then, are you? Every once in a while, I get stuck on a song that I know has potential, and Sam seems to know how to make them work."

"You'll always be welcome here," she said with a smile of her own.

They continued playing and singing through the morning, and then Sam called Chris Lancaster, Stan Bennet and Janice Peet and invited them over for what he called a very special lunch. Candy McAlester, the bass player, lived with Chris and would be arriving with him.

They all arrived shortly after noon, and found Sam on the back deck with burgers on the grill. They were all surprised to see Travis Bittner sitting there, but Sam brushed it off by saying Bittner had showed up begging for help in finishing off a song he was trying to write, and Bittner played along with the gag.

It wasn't until they had finished eating and were sitting around the picnic table sipping root beers that Sam called them to attention.

"Okay, guys," he began, "this isn't just a lunchtime get together. Travis flew in this morning because he got something important he wants to talk to you all about, and I thought getting you all together here was the best way to handle it." He turned to Bittner. "I think you ought to take it from there, don't you?"

Bittner put a smile on his face as he looked at the band. "I came to Sam first," he said, "because he's your front man. We talked this morning, and he's okay with what I'm about to propose, but it's something you each need to think about." He took a deep breath before he went on. "Country music is a big business, and it's not always easy to make it. I told Sam this morning that he's a very good singer, but he's not an incredible singer, and that's why I don't think he would find terrific success in Nashville."

Chris opened his mouth to speak, but Sam held out a hand. "Hold on," he said. "Just hear the rest of what he's got to say."

"Thanks, Sam. Look, guys, and girls, I've discovered a new singer. She's got the talent, she's got the looks, and now she needs the music behind her, and for the style she's developed, I can't find a better band than you guys. Like I said, I've already talked this over with Sam and he's okay with it. If you're all interested, and I do mean all of you, I'm ready to sign you to contract today. You will be the new girl's band, you'll spend the next couple of months in rehearsals and studio cutting an album, and then you'll be on tour for eight months after that. You will start out with her as my opening act, but by next year she'll be out on her own with you guys, and you'll all be topping the charts."

It took a full minute before anyone was able to

speak, and then they all tried to talk at once. There were some initial protests about leaving Sam, but Sam shut those down quickly. "Look, guys," he said, "I've had a lot of fun singing with you, but Travis is right. You guys are great, you're a great band, and you need a great singer out front. That just isn't me, and we all know it."

"But, Sam," Chris began, but Sam cut him off.

"Chris, stop. Being a singer was just a hobby for me, but music is what you guys are all about. Me? I'm a private eye, that's what I am. But you guys, you are professional musicians. Some of the best I've ever heard, by the way, and I'm glad that someone like Travis Bittner agrees with me on that."

There were a few more feeble protests, but it was pretty much a done deal at that point. Bittner looked at Sam and smiled, and the conversation turned to negotiating points in the contracts. Sam leaned back in his chair and sipped his root beer, and his wife pulled her own chair over close enough to lean her head on his shoulder.

"So," she whispered, "you really ready to give up the music business?"

"Yeah, I think I am. It's been fun, but it really isn't me. Besides, all the applause in the world can't compare to the thrills I've gotten when I've solved a case, maybe saved a life." He turned and looked at her. "What about you? Are you okay with this decision?"

"Oh, yes," Indie said. "It was a lot of fun at first, but some of those late nights really got to me." She looked at their friends, the members of what was likely to be the hottest new band in Nashville. "Besides," she went on, "we can always say we knew them when, right?"

Sam slipped an arm around her shoulders and pulled her close. "That we can, my love," he said. "That we can."

FOR BOOK 12

Check Availability At:
WWW.DAVIDARCHERBOOKS.COM

ABOUT

David Archer was born and raised in Bakersfield, California. He is a fiction author and novelist, writing in the mysteries and thrillers genre. His approach to writing is to hit deep, keep you entertained, and leave you wanting MORE with every turn of the page. He writes mysteries, thrillers, and suspense novels, all of which are primed to get your heart pumping.

The author's books are a mixture of mystery, action, suspense, and humor. If you're looking for a good place to start, take a look at his bestselling Sam Prichard Novels, available now. You can grab copies in eBook, Audio, or Paperback on all major retailers.

44356593R00148

Made in the USA
Middletown, DE
04 June 2017